THE LIGHT

THE LIGHT

BATTLE BETWEEN GOOD AND EVIL

By Reginald J. Williams

Order this book online at www.trafford.com
or email orders@trafford.com

Most Trafford titles are also available at major online book retailers.

Printed in the United States of America.

ISBN: 978-1-4669-0835-2 (sc)
ISBN: 978-1-4669-0836-9 (e)

Trafford rev. 01/11/2012

 www.trafford.com

North America & international
toll-free: 1 888 232 4444 (USA & Canada)
phone: 250 383 6864 ♦ fax: 812 355 4082

For Jabari Jr., Reggie III, Jarrel,
Nigel, Mattox and Joshua

ACKNOWLEDGEMENTS

I WANT TO thank those of you who have encouraged and cajoled me to continue and not give up. To those of you who snatched me out of the realm of procrastination and put foot to butt, "Stop watching the game and write". And to all of you who sat through my nagging of, "Hey, what do you think of this and does that make sense, and of course, read this and tell me what you think.

Thank you so very much, Alice, Asha, Ashlay, Cathleen, Dave M., Delano, Dianne, Faye, Fenella, Jabari, Jabo, John M., Kaye, Lily, Lisa, Malika, Margo, Mom, Pat, Reggie Jr., Ronisha, Sharon, and Sparky.

INTRODUCTION

THIS WAS A labor of love, a promise made to myself a long time ago. An oath I took to spin a tale outlining the choices that we make in life and their effect not only on others, but more importantly on our own psyche. Not a day goes by that we are not confronted with decisions as to which course of action we will choose, most of these decisions are mundane, every day, run-of-the-mill, choices decided upon without much thought or consternation—Fruit Loops or Coco Puffs for breakfast; do I go to the gym or Taco Bell. But every now and then we may have to sweat-out a more complex scenario that can tug at the very fabric of our ethical and moral constitution—Should I return this found wallet, and do so with all the money intact; how about tweaking my tax return with a few non-existing deductions and create my own stimulus package.

Sometimes the choices that require a conscious decision will have far greater consequences then the norm. These are the serious crossroads choices that are life-altering; one could even say they come under the perimeters of right and wrong or in the more serious cases "Good vs. Evil". These choices often outline how you will be perceived as a person by not only others, but how you view yourself as an individual.

It has been my goal to spin this particular saga with a little humor, some historical references, and above all a smidgen of horror acting as the rue to thicken this gumbo of a fairy tale. Hopefully the after-taste will linger long enough to cause you a moment of pause the next time you are faced with that big decision. Do I or Don't I

Or, you could just flip a coin.

Chapter 1

ENTER THE LIGHT

THE AMBULANCE WAS westbound on Wilshire Blvd. and doing at least 50 miles per hour, the wide eyed and erotically aroused first responder behind the wheel was thinking to himself—this is utterly bitching, damn near as good as sex as he then loudly recited his favorite quote from the movie 'Top Gun'; "I feel the need, the need for speed". This was indeed his favorite time of the shift, the pre-dawn early morning hours where traffic was virtually non-existent. The absence of vehicular and pedestrian traffic gave him the opportunity to drive the emergency ambulance balls to the wall like a bat out of hell. And even though it was against department policy to drive faster than the posted speed limit, he now had the large box shaped ambulance well past 35 and was fast approaching 60 miles per hour.

The emergency lights illuminating and reflecting off the storefront and office building windows added to the illusionary scenario of a great aerial combat being acted out in the EMT driver's mind. The eardrum piercing high-low wail of the siren and air horn echoed and reverberated through out the Wilshire Blvd. corridor. The high center-of-gravity caused the ambulance to sway back and forth as it barreled down the boulevard resulting in the driver's partner in the rear to be tossed about as she attempted to attend to their patient who was strapped on the gurney. "Slow your fat ass down" she yelled, "How are we gonna explain how this guy survived one accident only to be totaled in another one on the way to the hospital. I'm shit full of you playing twelve o'clock high with my life and career, slow it down."

Her partner just smiled as he increased the ambulance's speed. During normal business hours the siren's wail would have traffic pulling over to the right and pedestrians scampering back on the curb, but at this hour the warning devices attracted the attention of no one other than a small cadre of the homeless who had taken up their nocturnal residencies in the doorways and alley accesses in the after hour deserted businesses. Their reaction was one of annoyance other than anything else; after all they would be rousted out of their temporary shelters by various security personnel in just a few hours.

The driver could see the outline of Good Sam silhouetted in the distant, he readjusted in his seat then reached to turn off the emergency switches pretending he was lowering the landing gear and lining up his F-15 Tomcat for a two-wire night carrier landing. "You're looking good Maverick," he imagined the landing officer radioing, "Roger that, Maverick has the ball" he whispered just loud enough for his partner to hear and look up in digest. One minute later the ambulance came to a screeching halt at the emergency room entrance to Good Samaritan Hospital.

Paul figured they must have finally arrived at the emergency room. Even that good looking, blonde paramedic who wore that tight fitting zippered jumpsuit like she had been poured into it, had quit telling him that everything was going to be alright and to hang in there buddy. "Yeah right! Like I was going somewhere; what did she think I was going to do, jump up and break out in the electric slide in the back of the ambulance. Jesus H. Christ, those firefighters had spent nearly thirty minutes cutting me out of my new Porsche Carrera, no, make that my brand new $160,518.18 Porsche Carrera Cabriolet, arctic silver color rolling on Euromeister aluminum alloy wheels, Bose satellite surround sound system with GPS navigation and a lo-jack rip-off recovery package, the works baby. But she was no match for that dinosaur looking jaws-of-life tool the Los Angeles Fire Department unleashed on her".

"After they finally pulled me out, little Ms. Sexy Paramedic and her chubby unshaven partner who appeared to be sporting a hard-on that a cat couldn't scratch, strapped me down on a backboard complete with head and neck demobilization, cinched it to a gurney and shoved the whole contraption into the back of their ambulance". Paul could even swear he heard the chubby guy with the boner say something about needing speed and calling for some guy named Maverick.

"Hang in there, no shit baby I'm hanging big time, you guys got me hog-tied like a Thanksgiving turkey, I'm here for the duration". Paul struggled to amuse himself as was his relief mechanism for handling stressful situations. But suddenly a new feeling ambushed that stress relieving mechanism and forced it into the recesses of Paul's subconscious under the heading of; "To be continued later". A strange new sensation took over, Paul realized that he could no longer hear the blonde paramedic or her partner, he couldn't hear the hum of the ambulance's engine, matter-of-fact he could not hear anything what so ever, nothing, nada, zip.

He also then realized that he had no sensation of the outside world. What he did realize was that the pain in his leg was gone and that his head didn't hurt anymore. What the hell was going on here, it was the weirdest feeling he had ever experienced, but strangely not an unsettling feeling. Paul began to feel at ease almost euphoric, must be some damn good drugs Ms. Sexy Para-hottie is pushing thru that I.V., he mused.

Thelma stood staring at the elderly gentleman sitting behind an old wooden desk situated in the center of the large cream colored room; the only other piece of furniture was the swivel chair he was sitting on. But how had she gotten here; one second I was surrounded by nothing but total blackness that then transformed into a corridor of the most intense light that one could imagine. And then in a flash I'm standing in the middle of this eerie looking room staring at this odd but distinguishing looking old dude shoveling papers across a funky, beat-up piece of shit, desk. The old man had a head full of glimmering white hair with a matching mustache and a goatee. He was wearing a milky white suit with a white high buttoned collared shirt adorned with an off white silk tie and matching hankie. Thelma surmised that old pops probably had on white shoes and socks hidden from her field of view behind that desk. She also thought if this dude doesn't look like that Mark Twain cat that wrote Tom Finn Huckleberry Sawyer or whatever the name of that book was, my name ain't Thelma Johnson. The only problem was this dude was a brother. A black man wearing all that white, homey must have issues, she further surmised.

It was at that moment before she could utter a sound; the old man looked up and said "I ain't the one that just got caught on the wrong end of a drive-by, Homey! Now that's what I would call an issue and by the way Missy, Mr. Twain or more appropriately Mr. Samuel Clemens, penned the classic novels 'Tom Sawyer and Huckleberry Finn' they are two very distinct and different characters". Any other time Thelma might have soiled her pants, but she also had been overcome by that feeling of contentment and euphoria.

Crazy old man, I'm even more confused now then when I first saw him sitting behind that desk. "No matter," James muttered under his breath, "I will figure this out for heaven's sake, after all I am a Harvard Law School graduate. I didn't become the youngest associate partner of Shuster, Haynes, and Smith's Investment Firm by accident, oh yeah I can handle this." James began to take inventory of the events that led up to this moment. Now let's see he calculated, I just left the morning board meeting, tough meeting yes but I did ok, walked to the elevator, door closed, then something; the sharp chest pains and dizziness, it was coming back in total clarity now. Just before he thought he'd pass out the elevator door opened to revel the darkest night he had ever seen, but how that was possible didn't make sense, it was what 10:30, 10:45 in the morning at the latest. He remembered thinking that the dark void was reacting like a living entity and wanted to hitch a ride to the lobby. James also remembered being bewildered and perplexed by these events but not afraid, he even started to experience a sense of contentment. It was as if all is well with the world.

Paul, Thelma Mae, and even James had all heard of 'The Light', it was that often spoke of brilliant glow that many witnessed at the beginning of their demise. Don't walk into the light, stay away from the light, Thelma and Paul remembered those lines from the movie 'Poltergeist', that little girl Carol Ann didn't walk into the light and everything turned out just fine for her. James, who never went to the movies or watched much television couldn't recall where he had exactly heard about the result of taking that illuminant stroll, but he also had an inclination that to remain in the land of the living, that was not the desired direction. But sometimes what you know makes no difference; the compulsion to comply was just too overwhelming. Ever so slowly, he stepped into the brilliance.

Paul's light encounter manifested itself moments after the siren stopped. The back of the ambulance door slowly opened up to that black void and what started out as a small pinpoint of light began to grow and intensify to the point where it was all consuming and as much as Paul was reluctant, he did manage to unfasten his restraints, get up from the gurney and walk without the slightest bit of pain straight into the middle of the brilliant glow.

James was still trying to rationalize the chest pains, the strange elevator ride, and why he had so easily succumbed to the compulsion to stroll into the brilliant but non-blinding brightness when he noticed the old man sitting at the desk. "Sir if I may ask where I am" he began, "Shhh . . .", the old man said without looking up "I think you know what's going on here you just refuse to acknowledge it. But trust me, do as I say and all your questions will be answered. Walk through that door over there and follow the path were you will come to a small pond, once there have a seat and wait. Just remember to stay your journey and speak to no one, not until you arrive at the pond." "But but..," "No buts" the old man interjected "On your way now get", he said pointing to the door.

Thelma listened intently as the old man gave her directions to the pond, she did not have a formal college education but Thelma was as bright as they come, common sense, street smarts, and a no nonsense demeanor; she was a strong, confident, independent, black woman who did not have to depend on anyone for anything. Thelma suddenly recalled hearing the screech of the SUV's tires as they raced down the street toward her front yard, what she had not heard but now remember hearing was the sound of the machine pistol that opened up as she was getting out of her car upon returning home from work.

Chapter 2

"G" AND THE CREW

"TAKE THAT BITCH", Lil G the west side's youngest major drug and gang leader shouted, as the gold colored Cadillac Escalade sped off burning rubber down the street barely missing three young children that elderly Miss Emma was escorting across the avenue. The SUV took the corner on two wheels with its spinning style hubcaps furiously rotating and glistening under the street lamp then dissipated into the night. Lil G stuffing the Mack-10 automatic pistol under the back seat leaned back and smiled, "I warned that do-gooder bitch for the last time; she won't be dissin me or snitching to Five-O bout my business no more".

Lil G born Gerald Lee Henderson had started Too Little Crew, the name of his posse when he was only fourteen years old. What had began as a tiny block gang had grown into Inglewood's toughest and most brutal street organization in just eight years. Becoming knee deep in drugs, extortion, intimation, rape, and murder, Too Little Crew or "TLC", as they were known had all of Inglewood and a large portion of West Los Angeles under its thumb. And their leader Lil G, an intelligent but totally ruthless young man ruled with an iron fist. It seemed that the police or Five-O, as the gangsters called them were always one step behind, they were definitely out numbered and often times out gunned. The public knowing this, would never ever volunteer any info that would be beneficial in bringing these thugs to justice, fear of retaliation had stayed the tongue of everyone in Inglewood, everyone except Thelma Johnson.

Thelma Mae Johnson was an attractive thirty-five year old black woman with what most would call an attitude. Thelma didn't take shit from anybody; it didn't matter if it was her supervisors at the post office where she worked the swing shift or her ex-husband Ronald Johnson, whom she had given the boot to four years earlier for his crack cocaine and alcohol addiction, not to mention his excessive extramarital affairs.

So surely Lil G and his gangbanging junior flips perpetrating their nefarious activities in the neighborhood did not scare her one damn bit. "Lil G my ass", she would often say to anyone within ear shot, "I remember that little bastard running around all snotty-nosed in his pee-stained diapers. His momma should have whipped that ass when he first started acting up". Her friends would tell her that it was probably a bad idea to bad-mouth these guys like she did, but Thelma was never one to bite her tongue especially when she saw a wrong that needed to be righted. She went so far as to call the police on more than one occasion, but not actually being an eyewitness to a felony offense, left the authorities with their hands tied.

Police or no police Thelma wasn't having it, just earlier that same day she had gotten in the face of Lil G and his posse over at Jesse Owens Park located not too far from her house. She had been on her way to work when she spotted the posse hanging out by the basketball courts, smoking pot, loud talking, and bullying the youngsters trying to play ball. Driving her Honda Accord over the curb, she bee-lined across the grass right at them sending the posse on an escape and evade in all directions. Thelma smiled as she thought they looked like roaches scrambling for cover when the kitchen light was turned on. Slamming the gear shift into park, she was out of the car before it came to a complete stop; hands on her hips and head bobbing the ghetto bounce, she screamed at Lil G so loud and fast that spit spray from those full thick southern girl lips peppered his face like tiny liquid machine gun bullets. "Who the hell you little bastards think you are" she shouted, "This park is for the neighborhood kids, they don't need to have to deal with you cowardly, gangbanging, wanna-be hoodlums, peddling dope and bothering decent people. You all should be ashamed of yourselves". Her eyes darted back and forth between the posse members, "Can't you see you are only hurting our own people with these drugs".

"And you", looking at Lil G, "You knock-off Scarface, Neno Brown wanna-be," getting nose to nose with the young thug, "These children already got two strikes against them just trying to survive and make something of themselves; and they see you and these other ass wipes running around high all the time, brandishing guns and acting like fools; what kind of example does that set". Lil G just stood there; he could not believe that this bitch had the nerve to get in his face like this.

The posse couldn't get a grip on what was unfolding before their eyes; they were absolutely mesmerized; it was as though time itself had come to a complete standstill. They didn't know rather to shit or go blind, the safest thing was not to react until Lil G did. Their eyes switched back and forth between G and Thelma who were still standing nose to nose in their Ali vs. Frazier standoff. Neither would budge, the stare down was intense enough to put Dirty Harry to shame; then suddenly Thelma spun around, hopped into the Honda, gunned the engine, slammed the transmission into drive, and fished-tailed toward the street. The gravel and grass being kicked up by the rear tires and thrown into the faces of the posse shook them out of their hypnotic trance and again sent them on that roach scramble. Lil G just stood there unflinching still frozen in the moment; jaw tight and left eye twitching furiously he glared at the Honda's tail lights fading down the street.

"Mouthy ass bitch your day is coming," he whispered. "Fuck that" he suddenly yelled, "Tonight yeah tonight, I know what time your bitch-ass gets off work". Lil G's jaw eased its tension and a sinister little smirk appeared.

and would never roll over for anybody, he had worked hard to earn his reputation and to wimp out to some thug was out of the question, what ever happens will happen he said to himself.

Just as Paul hit a twenty foot jumper to end the game and G and his boys started to walk on the court; the Inglewood Police Department's basketball team strolled in the gym in full force. They were wearing their green warm-up suits and baseball caps with the IPD logo in matching green and white letters. They also had their holstered department issued Glock nines and ammo belts hanging over their shoulders, a couple of the officers even had shotguns tucked under their arms as they made their way along the gym wall to the bleachers. It was department policy not to leave weapons locked in their vehicles when in certain areas that had a history of police vehicle break-ins.

Inglewood's finest had come to the park to get some practice in before the up-coming California Police and Firemen's Summer Olympics Games that was to be held the following week. Leading the officers and sipping on a large Starbucks was homicide detective L. Z. Anderson the team coach, he leaned the shotgun against the bleacher seat, looked around then hollered out, "**We Got Next**".

Lil G staring out the passenger window as they drove down Hyde Park Ave. knew he would cross paths with that white boy again. Yeah, next time we'll see who'll be floatin, he thought as a sinister grin appeared on his face.

Chapter 4

Pro Ball

Paul went on to lead Westchester High to the state championship his senior year before enrolling at Long Beach State on a full athletic scholarship and even though academics was not one of his strong attributes, he managed to complete his freshman and sophomore years before the lure of the NBA became just too strong to ignore.

Managers and would-be agents knowing full well that it was against NCAA rules; were still clandestinely beating his door down to represent his interest in turning pro. Hardly a day went by without some representative from a sport agency slipping him a business card and whispering how much money was waiting if he just signed on the dotted line. They said the opportunities for a good-looking, clean-cut, white ball player that played the so called street brand of basketball, were astronomical; a player like that could write his own ticket. As one sport agent so bluntly stated; "Paul Logan is a Larry Bird, with Michael Jordan moves and Magic Johnson court leadership". Paul had always hated the black vs. white comparison when it came to sports, all he knew was that he loved playing ball and if you had game it didn't matter what color you were.

But the NBA and playing professional basketball had always been Paul's ultimate goal; it would provide an opportunity for him to take care of his mother Lucy and his two younger sisters Pam and Karen. He had promised to buy them a new house, put both girls through school and to make sure his mother didn't have to work another day in her life. She had slaved at two jobs just to make ends meet ever since Paul's father Jeffrey Logan had mysteriously disappeared when Paul was only ten years old. He supposedly had gone to the Normandie Club in Gardena to play poker one evening and was never heard from again. The police had no leads or clues and the disappearance went unsolved. After seven years Jeffrey was declared legally deceased and Lucy was officially a widow.

That was five years ago, since then Lucy had been both mother and father, it was a struggle but Paul and his sisters never wanted for anything. As far as Paul was concerned, she was the best mom in the world and his number one fan; he loved her dearly.

The week after Long Beach State had been eliminated in the NCAA Basketball Western Conference Finals losing to the University of Arizona 87-86, Paul chose an agent and became available for the NBA draft. Just as predicated, he was selected in the first round by the Los Angeles Clippers and just as he promised, he purchased his mother a brand new home in Pacific Palisades. He also set up a generous trust fund for his sisters before purchasing himself a brand new Porsche Carrera Cabriolet sports car with all the trimmings.

Swish all net, the second free throw was just as successful as the first. The capacity crowd went berserk as the Clippers won behind Floatin Logan's 31st and 32nd points on two game winning free throws. "Not bad for a rookie", Paul boasted to himself as the team headed for the locker room, not bad at all for a skinny white boy from Westchester. Next step the five S's; shit, shower, shave, shine, and shampoo, before hopping in the babe magnet and driving over to Little J's for a little party time, he smiled and whispered to himself, "I'm definitely getting laid tonight".

Chapter 5

BIG JAMES

JAMES WAS SO relaxed laying by the pond that he actually nodded off a couple of times and as strange as this whole experience was playing out, he actually felt like the pressures of the corporate world had faded into oblivion. "I guess I'm just chillin", he smiled to himself. James Pettigrew III was never one to use slang, local colloquialisms, and by no means ever any form of Ebonics, James L. Pettigrew Sr., James' grandfather or "Big James" as he was known by the family, had stressed the importance of using the king's proper English to his children and grandchildren. James' father, James Pettigrew Jr. not only instilled this into his son but also extolled the virtues of proper etiquette and social graces as well. "Just chillin, father would just die if he heard me saying that, hell he'd come strolling out of that white light, Son what did you say" . . . "Yo! Pops cop a squat and chill-out," James imagined himself saying, he began to laugh so hard he couldn't see straight.

The Pettigrews were one of the more influential and wealthiest black families in the Los Angeles area. Big James Pettigrew had come to Los Angeles right after World War II and opened up a soul food restaurant on 42nd and Central Ave. right across the street from the now famous and then popular Dunbar Hotel where all the black entertainers and entrepreneurs stayed when they were in town.

emphasis on education. Patricia and Faye Pettigrew each earned their MBAs from Stanford and Columbia University respectfully and James Jr. graduated first in his class from Harvard University's School of Law. It was never any question where James III would attend college or what field he would pursue. The Pettigrews wanted a lawyer in the family. James III could specialize in whatever branch of law he wanted, but he was going to be a Harvard educated attorney; so said his father and so said both of his aunts. But young James never had a taste for the criminal aspects of the law, arguing guilt or innocence, prosecuting or defending the accused just wasn't how he wished to live his life. Business Law was where he would make his mark; representing high-end rich clients, real estate acquisitions, corporate takeovers, rubbing shoulders with the major movers and shakers was the way to climb right to the top. The money was good but power and prestige is what he craved more, young James had a burning desire to show his aunts and his father that he had the mettle to become a big success. But even this was secondary to his real goal; to impress his grandfather.

Young James had tried to get his grandfather's approval and admiration his whole life, but with little success it seemed. Big James Sr. was not an easy man to impress nor did he shower accolades on his children or grandchildren at the drop of a hat, it was as if their high achievements were expected, anything less was met with a wanting explanation of why and a question of commitment and dedication.

This didn't seem to bother either his father or his aunts; they were secure in their achievements and their own self worth. Their attitude was, you do your thing and we'll do ours. Young James could not really ever recall his family discussing their private affairs with Big James. They did not want or need Big James' approval or blessings on anything they did. But James III was going to show everyone who the real success in this family was.

James III had made associate partner at "Shuster, Haynes and Smith" based on his acquisition of one hundred acres of prime developmental real estate in the west Los Angeles area located near Los Angeles International

Airport. Not only did he have to convince three of Southern California's major financial institutions to invest one hundred million dollars each to bankroll this LAX project, but he persuaded the partners of the firm to guarantee a ten percent return on the investment within one year of signing on with the project. That came to thirty million dollars that "Shuster, Haynes and Smith" would have to shell out of their own coffers if things bogged down or heaven forbid went belly-up due to a lack of predevelopment sales to potential tenants.

The pressure of getting this huge residential/commercial endeavor financed, zoned, environmentally approved and under construction was taking a toll on young James; it seemed as if one problem after another was the rule rather than the exception. Cost overruns, labor disputes and construction set-backs are problems James was prepared to deal with. But a different concern was manifesting itself that could torpedo the project in its tracks.

Crime was on the rise on the Westside, gang activity and drugs to be precise and this had the investors on a high-speed wobble. It seemed that this young vicious group of thugs who called themselves "Too Little Crew" was the new criminal element in town, led by a young local gangster who called himself "Lil G".

They were intent on expanding their influence beyond Inglewood and to control the drug trade west of the San Diego Freeway from Westwood on the north to Manhattan Beach on the south. They were young, aggressive, well financed and totally ruthless.

The big money boys were concerned that business was going to suffer immensely if the situation went unchecked. They had seen this in other parts of the city over the years, East L.A., South Central, the San Gabriel Valley, even Palmdale which is located forty miles northwest of the city on the edge of the high desert. It didn't matter where or who resided in these areas, once drugs and the gang element got a toe hold it took time for law enforcement to regain control, if they ever did. In the meantime the local economy took a big slide, property values dropped like winter temperatures, and law abiding citizens chose to take their business elsewhere.

Of course this situation had the attention of Charles Shuster, Arnold Haynes and Osgood Smith or the "Three Wise Men", as they were know as by the firm's employees. They shuttered at the possibility of having to make good on that thirty million dollar good faith guarantee that James Pettigrew had talked them into endorsing. So the three of them as a group and individually let James know how disappointed, no make that very disappointed they would be if this current course of events did not correct itself before the proverbial "Shit hit the fan", if just one of the big money investors ran scared, a trickle down effect would be in full swing and the firm most definitely did not want to take that thirty million dollar hit.

That was the main topic of the morning meeting; James had to explain to the wise men and the investors what was being done to insure the success of the project. Hard questions were being asked, these big dollar jockeys wanted iron-clad assurances that the crime aspect was going to disappear forthwith and that the project was on schedule. James had no idea how to deal with this gang and drug element, law enforcement couldn't provide a creditable timetable as to when order would be restored and he had nowhere else to turn. Sure he could mislead, befuddle and baffle the board with bullshit for a short time but if he didn't produce results soon, the "Three Wise Men" would replace him with one of the firm's more experienced sharp-shooters and James knew that would mark the end of his career at Shuster, Haynes and Smith.

But the deepest cut of all, he would be viewed as a failure by the family and by his grandfather; that was a dreaded fate worse than death.

After the meeting James felt like crap, the knot in his stomach was throbbing and pulsating like nobody's business and his chest was experiencing a vise grip tightening that nearly brought him to his knees. He was barely able to push the elevator button. He then half walked and stumbled inside when the door opened. Then that black void followed by the bright light.

Chapter 6

ALLIANCES

PAUL WAS THINKING that old dude must be out of his ever-lovin mind but the old man in the Colonel Sanders suit was adamant about taking this path to a pond where all his questions would be answered, yeah right he thought; "Dude must think my name is Willy Foo Fool or something. One minute I'm driving to the club, the next this gold Escalade comes out of nowhere and bang, I'm in an ambulance on my way straight to the Twilight Zone". Paul was still trying to figure out why that Caddy Escalade was high-tailing from the cops before it did the accordion job on his Porsche when he saw the man in the Brooks Brothers suit stretched out under a willow tree next to the most serene little pond he had ever seen. "Yo bro, you the dude supposed to explain this nightmare to me or what", he yelled.

"I beg your pardon sir", a startled James said quickly rising from under the willow tree. "First off, I am not of any relation to you sir let along your brother and as far as an explanation is concerned, I to am in a quandary as to the course of events to which we are a party". Paul looking at James like he was from another planet asked, "Does that mean you don't know what the fuck is going on either" "Watch your language sir" James replied, "And to answer your crudely stated response, I am also in the dark why I, excuse me, we are here. The elderly gentleman alluded to the possibility that answers would be provided upon my arrival at this location. But judging by your previous outburst I suspect that you are not the individual that can provide said explanation". "You gotta be shittin me" Paul snickered at James' response, "Who put that bug up your ass. Look bro, oh excuse me, look mister, I'm not looking for trouble I'm just trying to get a grip on what the hell is going on here, feel me".

Thelma walking gingerly on the path the old man had pointed out heard voices up ahead. As she rounded the corner she stopped and stared at a perplexing scene. This rather well dressed brother was arguing with this tall, young white guy. She was perplexed to say the least because the black guy was talking like he had just stepped off the boat from jolly ole England while the white dude sounded and acted like one of the brothers who lived on her block.

"You two gonna stop yakking at each other and tell me what the hell is going on here". Paul and James both were startled at the sound of Thelma's voice. "Damn, you nearly made me shit my pants" Paul gasped "Don't be sneaking up on folks like that." "Oh so elegantly stated" James chimed in; "I beg your pardon Miss but are you privy as to what our current situation entails". "Huh," Thelma uttered. "Yeah see, that's what I'm dealing with here lady," Paul shouted. "Nobody can understand what this asshole is talking about; privy, entails, what in good goddamn does that mean, son-of-a-bitch ain't making sense." "Please control yourself you uncouth barbarian and again watch your language, there's a lady present," James shot back. "Hey Jeeves, I can see that the sister is a lady, but she can't figure out what your nerdy ass is saying either." "Both of you shut up" Thelma said forcibly, "It's obvious that the three of us are in the same boat, we are all stuck here in Bizzarro World and arguing among ourselves is not going to help matters one bit, I suggest that we all calm down and introduce ourselves then try to figure out what's going on and what to do about it."

"My name is Thelma Johnson." "I feel you sister; I'm Paul, Paul Logan nice to meet you." "Oh I know you;" Thelma said "You're that basketball player just drafted by the Clippers, from Long Beach State, right." "Oh snap" Paul said "You follow B-Ball, right-on." "I should have known" James butted in, "Another uneducated, over paid, pampered, professional gladiator." "Hey dude" Paul responded, "You can kiss my over paid, pampered, uneducated . . ." Thelma cut in, "Now that's not necessary . . . Mr?" "Pettigrew, James Pettigrew the third" James said, "And you are most certainly correct Ms. Johnson, I sir apologize please forgive my outburst" he said looking at Paul; "I will in the future attempt to be more courteous." "James Pettigrew the third" Paul snickered, "You mean that you are the third in a line of stuck up assholes. Please don't have any kids, the world as we know it would definitely end with the birth of a James Pettigrew the fourth." "Now now" Thelma interjected, "Mr. Pettigrew did say he was sorry." "Please call me James Ms. Johnson;" "And you can call me Thelma," she answered as they both looked at Paul. Paul looking them both up and down said "And you can call me a cab out of this nightmare."

Chapter 8

Big Spooky

Lil G sitting in the back seat could remember yelling at Tray as they sped through downtown Los Angeles, with the LAPD in hot pursuit. "Drive the car mofo shit, if they stop us with these Macks under the seat we go down for popping that do-gooder bitch. And if they find the two keys of blow in the trunk, we ain't never gonna see the streets again. I'm not going away for life cause your stupid ass can't drive worth a damn". Racing north on Figueroa Blvd. posse member Tray had the gold Escalade doing eighty as they sped passed the Staple Center, weaving in and out of the remnants of traffic that was heading home from the various late night party venues in downtown Los Angeles. "Take a left on 9th Street" G shouted, "But that's a one-way we'll be headed against traffic", Tray protested. "Dumb ass I know it's a one-way, the cops will have back off maybe we can make it to the freeway or at least give me a chance to dump these Macks without being seen". Tray hit the corner at 9th and Figueroa going westbound dodging eastbound traffic as best he could, Smiley riding shotgun in the front seat next to Tray was doing the best Mantan Morland, Stepin Fetchit impression ever seen. His eyes were big as saucers and he had a vise-like grip on the dashboard. Then he started screaming like a Harlem-sissy in the men's lockup at Parker Center Jail. Just as Tray looked over to tell Smiley to shut the hell up a silver-gray Porsche came out of nowhere.

Lil G slowly opened his eyes expecting to see either Tray or Smiley, no driving assholes of all the homeboys on the Westside I end up with these two inept motherfuckers, can't you do anything right G began to shout out. What he saw stopped him in mid-sentence. He was standing in the middle of a large room or so it seemed, the walls were a strange pinkish red color and didn't seem to be solid at all but kind of a transparent misty configuration, there was no ceiling as one would normally describe but a reddish mist that was solid and not solid at the same time.

There were no windows or doors anywhere and no sound of any kind, damn strange Lil G was thinking but he also felt a sense of ease and well-being like he belonged in this place, like he was supposed to be here, like he had been waiting his whole life to get here. Then he noticed the shadowlike figure standing in the corner behind him.

Lil G was looking at a tall, strange looking figure moving toward him; it was as if he wasn't walking but kind of gliding like on air. He was wearing a long, dusty grey colored robe with a hood. G thought damn if he doesn't remind me of that Grim Reaper dude, only this cat wasn't carrying that big sickle-blade thing but he did have what appeared to be a large black folder tucked under his right arm. The closer he got to G the taller and more ominous he became, he stood at least seven feet maybe more Lil G surmised, it was hard to tell with that robe-hoody garment hanging off the dude. The drab attire went from head to ground but the most disturbing thing was that Lil G could not see a face inside that hood. All that was there was a black void that seemed to go on forever; looking into that hood was akin to staring into some strange, timeless abyss. There were no physical features what so ever, also there were no signs of any limbs even at the end of the sleeves where hands were supposed to be, there was nothing. It was as if this seven-foot gray robe was wrapped around black empty space shaped like a tall humanoid figure.

It stopped and hovered right in front of Lil G looking down at him; what happened next made the fearless leader of Too Little Crew quiver on the spot like a cornered jackrabbit negotiating his next move while staring up the snarling snout of a California Mountain Lion. The figure spoke but no sound came from where one would guess his mouth would be; instead the words just resounded in Lil G's head. It was a deep resonating and foreboding tone. **"You were summoned"**

Chapter 9

THE MISSIONS

LIL G WAS starting to get used to big spooky's mode of communication, in fact he thought it was kind of cool the words just seemed to appear in his head. And he considered it a double bonus that he didn't have to mouth his own words. "Hey big Homey" G mentally expressed, "What's in the black notebook under your arm". "**Your destiny**" was the mental reply, with that the black folder started to levitate and float from under the arm of the giant figure. As it slowly glided toward Lil G, it opened up and hovered just a few inches from his face. What he saw made him shudder with pure hatred and utter contempt. There he was staring at three 8x10 color photos of Thelma Mae Johnson, Paul "Floatin" Logan, and James Pettigrew III.

Lil G was so taken back; he forgot that he didn't have to physically mouth his words. "What's that Miss-Goody-Two-Shoes and that basketball playing white boy have to do with me", he shouted at the tall figure. "And who's the suit" he asked referring to James Pettigrew, "I ain't ever seen him before". "**Your destiny**" again was the reply. "My destiny, what the fuck does that mean, matter of fact where the hell am I, what am I doing here, where's Tray and Smiley". Lil G now extremely agitated was screaming at the top of his lungs. At that moment the resonating sound in Lil G's head became so loud and vibrant that it brought him to his knees. "**Your destiny, accept it or view your fate**" was ringing loud, clear, and in perfect pitch through every nerve synapse in Lil G's brain. With that the tall figure pointed his left abnormally long robed covered arm to the far wall; as Lil G spun around on his knees what he saw sent a feeling of terror and horror so intense through his entire being that he thought he would go completely mad at any moment.

There in the corner of the room was Tray and Smiley each naked as the day they were born, both were engulfed in a circle of white hot flame. Their skin was bubbling and pulsating as it began to melt off each of their bodies. The pair obviously in excruciating pain were screaming and wailing for mercy. Lil G tried as hard as he could to turn away from the horrific sight but was unable to divert his eyes. It was as though each one of his posse members were encapsulated in his own private cocoon of hell itself.

Their screams were deafening and the vision so gruesome that the ruthless gang leader was reduced to a quivering mass of helplessness. "Please make it stop, oh God please make it stop". "**He won't help you**", was the mental reply. And just like that, Tray and Smiley were gone. "**Your fate or your destiny, the choice is yours**" was the last thought Lil G had before he passed out.

Paul, Thelma, and James stood in a semi-circle around Gus looking at each other with a mutually agreeable expression on their faces. "Ok we're down" Paul extorted, "What's next". Gus smiled thinking to himself, maybe the boss was right they may just work out after all. "Ok here's the deal" Gus began, "The three of you are going back where you will find each other and figure out a way to stop Lil G and his plans to bring corruption and mayhem to Los Angeles. It will be up to you three to protect the innocent from his insidious evil endeavors. How you accomplish this task is your mission". "No problem" Paul said, "We find the little bastard and put one in his ear, game over". "Whoa time out there superstar", Gus said giving Paul the referee T-shape hand signal, "You can't kill him. Remember he's in the same transitional phase that you are, plus that's really not how we handle things on our side".

"Well hell, what are we supposed to do use harsh language and give him a time-out", Paul shouted. "We can't kill him because he's dead already and what about us, I hope that shit works both ways". "Yes it does" Gus answered, "But unfortunately you can still be hurt and feel pain, nothing I can do about that. Just remember who you're dealing with here. This is not a ball game with rules and regulations to keep things fair and above board, the other side will not hesitate to do whatever. They will have no mercy and won't care who may get hurt in the process, never ever forget that".

"Mr. Gus" interjected James; "Let me make sure we have a full and accurate assessment of the situation. We as a group have to confront this G Little fellow and thwart his efforts in becoming the next major drug lord in Los Angeles. How we accomplish this is contingent upon our own resourcefulness; we cannot physically vanquish young Mr. G because he has previously met with his demise, as so with the three of us; plus doing so is not the preferred method employed by the powers that be which rule over this domain.

Are these not the facts". As Gus blinked repeatedly at James, Paul screamed "Jeez man lighten up, can't you speak so normal people can figure out at least half of what's coming out of your mouth. Pops here lives north of the Pearly Gates and even he doesn't know what the hell you saying". "Easy Paul" Thelma sighed, "Let Gus finish". Gus still staring at James, shook his head as though he was trying to get his ears and brain back in sync continued on. "Lil G and his followers will be ruthless, conniving and cunning. He will be unmerciful in his quest to achieve the goals set by his evil handlers. But there is an upside" Gus continued; "Those evil forces behind Lil G are not very patient, they want immediate results. If they do not get this immediate gratification they will not hesitate to remove Lil G; and when I say remove I mean he's going to face a fate to horrible to describe".

"Oh that's too bad my heart will really bleed for the little snot" laughed Thelma, "Me to", Paul chimed in. "What else old man, we gonna have super powers or something. I mean can we fly or walk through walls, read people's minds, do any of that Twilight Zone shit". "Fraid not" Gus said, "You will appear normal just like you did before you arrived here, you will be placed back at the moment of your transition. You Miss Johnson will be hearing from the police how fortunate you were that the bullets all missed. Mr. Pettigrew you can expect to reach the parking lot where the chest pains will be fading. And Mr. Logan everyone will marvel that the hit-and-run crash caused only a sprained ankle and sore back; injured just enough to go on the injured reserve list for the Clippers, you have a more important mission than scoring thirty points a game during the exhibition basketball season. I would suggest that the three of you get together as soon as possible and plan your course of action".

Lil G was shaking his head and trying to blink his eyes back into focus, right then he felt as though his whole life had been summed up in a one page essay with the three middle paragraphs missing. He could remember that horrible scene with Tray and Smiley, but how could that be. Wasn't that Tray driving with Smiley riding shotgun in the front seat of the Caddy. "Yo guys you alright". What G saw when Tray and Smiley turned around made the hairs on his arms and back of his neck stand erect and tingle like crazy. Both Tray and Smiley were burned almost beyond recognition; it seemed that their skin had melted and hardened into a most grotesque configuration.

They both smiled; at least G thought that they were smiling. Under what was left of each nose there were only teeth, both of the young gangsters' lips were completely burned off. They resembled a couple of hairless animated cartoon skulls with bug-eyes, chattering back and forth with each other. "We good to go G". They spoke and moved simultaneously, it was as though they were now somehow symbiotically linked. And they did not seem to either know or acknowledge their gruesome appearance.

Lil G still exorcising the cobwebs from his head began to recall the events leading up to this moment; the collision with the Porsche, the 8x10 photos, Big Spooky and his "**Fate or destiny speech**". It was all becoming alarmingly clear now. Somehow, someway he was back from the big beyond; back with a sense of invincibility and power. He felt he could do whatever he wanted. And what he wanted was to run this towns' drug trade; exclusively. But first he had to deal with the three amigos Big Spooky had targeted. No problem, he had no love for that bitch Thelma and even less for that ball playing white boy, and as far as the nerdy looking brother in the suit was concerned, he would merit special attention. But how to begin he wondered, Big Spooky did say that they were in the same boat; can't smoke them, but there are other ways Lil G smiled to himself. He picked up and patted the portfolio that Big Spooky had given him; this will come in handy, oh yeah very handy he growled under his breath. "Hey Tray, Smiley you two almost burn-up, crispy-critter, motherfuckers ready to put in some work".

Chapter 10

WE'RE BACK

Thelma was sitting in her living room on the edge of the sofa while the television echoed the local morning news in the background. She was trying to digest what the police officer who had showed up to take the shots fired report was saying. "Lady whoever did this was either trying to scare you or they are the most inept shooters alive, I mean they must have been wearing blindfolds. They hit everything but you, with a machine pistol nonetheless", the officer said. "Are you absolutely positive that you didn't recognize anyone". Thelma was tempted just for a microsecond to run the whole story down to the officer, but immediately realized that probably would not be a Summa Cum Laude idea. She figured if someone had told her a fantastic tale like that she would think they were either crazy or on crack.

At that moment the sportscaster on the Channel 7 News was reporting from Good Samaritan Hospital in downtown Los Angeles, the amazing story of how Clipper super rookie Paul Logan had survived a horrible hit and run accident the night before after leading his team to a come from behind victory over the Minnesota Timberwolves. His sports car was totaled but all he suffered was an ankle injury and a sore back, the team physician predicted Logan would be sidelined only three to four weeks, max. The police officer glancing at the television said, "Lady you and that basketball player have to be the two luckiest or blessed people in Los Angeles. A buddy of mine was in pursuit of the car that smashed into that guy last night, he said there was no way that ball player should have survived that crash. It's too bad the bastards that clipped him got away. You two must have the same guardian angel or something". Thelma had to bite her bottom lip to keep from chuckling out loud. "Thank you officer I have your card if I remember anything more I won't hesitate to call, but right now I have to visit a good friend in the hospital".

The elevator door opened to the underground parking garage, the rush of air though tinted with the smell of gasoline was refreshing to James. His chest pains had faded and the throbbing headache was subsiding to a dull slight discomfort.

While James adjusted his attire, Raul the parking attendant asked, "Mr. Pettigrew sir are you alright. Sir you're sweating something fierce". "Oh Raul" James answered, "Thank you but I'm fine. I believe the cuisine at Pierre's last night must not have agreed with me". James began to take inventory on the previous events. Had he imagined all this, was the dinner last night and the pressure he has been under really responsible for such an elaborate hallucination. His stomach did feel queasy; I know James thought to himself, Dr. George Robnet the family physician's office was not far. Dr. Robnet's office is just a couple of miles over at Good Sam, I'll take a chance he can squeeze me in for a quick check up, he's been after me to come in for months. At the very least maybe I can get a prescription for some valium or something, no problem I'll be fine he thought to himself.

Paul laying in the hospital bed was putting the finishing touches on a special autograph for Nancy the cute little night nurse who just adored professional athletes. "You can sponge bath me anytime, preferably at my place", signed Paul Floatin Logan, #33 in the program, #1 in your heart. Just then Thelma opened the door. "Oh excuse me they said you were alone". "Jeez Lady" Paul screamed, as the semi-woody under his hospital gown did a quick melt down. "Does not the sign on the door say private. Oh

pick-me-up, know what I mean". "Is that right" Lil G whispered, taking a sip of Hennessey. "What does that have to do with me". "Oh come on now young blood" Willie said while filling G's brandy snifter, "Everybody knows you the man". "Ok Willie for argument sake, say I am the man what can you do for me". "Blow young blood, I'm your go to guy, I know I can move enough flake to ski a slalom on, a brother just needs a little jump start to get the ball rolling. Now if you could see fit to front me say one key to start. I can pretty much guarantee you a handsome return on your generosity, I'm telling you G I couldn't fuck this up if I wanted to, it's a no-brainer, player". "Ok Willie" G said motioning for another shot of Hennessey; "You seem to be good people what kind of collateral we talking about". "Collateral" Willie asked, looking bewildered. "Sure, a kilo of pure unstepped on cocaine ain't cheap" G answered back, "I gotta have a little insurance, business is business. I mean Muhammad Ali paid for that haircut, didn't he". Big Willie laughed; "Sure he did young blood, fuckin-a-right he paid for it".

"I tell you what Willie; is this place paid for or mortgaged up the ying-yang". "The bar and grill" Willie countered, "This place is all mine lock, stock, and last rib bone, why". "You let me hold the paper on the bar and grill just as a show of good faith on your part; no big deal right. It shouldn't take more than say a month at most to move a funky kilo of blow. At the end of a month you pay me what you owe, I give you back the paper. No muss, no fuss, neither one of us can lose everybody's covered; beside you said no problems". Even though Big Willie felt the knot in his stomach tighten a little, he smiled at Lil G "Sure young blood no problem, deal. When we gonna make this happen". "I got the blow in the trunk of my car, where's the deed", Lil G answered back. Big Willie who was now feeling apprehensive yet excited at the same time opened his wall safe and handed over all his ownership papers to Lil G Henderson. "Here you go young blood let this happen".

In exactly one month to the day Big Willie Greene called Lil G on his cell and made arrangements to meet early the next Sunday morning in the bar and grill office to settle up accounts. Willie at first had a feeling that maybe he had made a big mistake trusting Lil G with the deed to the bar and grill, but G hadn't pressured him at all the previous month, matter of fact he'd had only showed up a few times to shoot pool and to knock down some ribs. He hardly spoke to Willie let alone say anything about their business endeavor. A couple of times though G had this Mr. Peabody looking brother named Quincy something or other with him, remembered Willie. He thought this Quincy guy didn't quite fit in with G's normal posse members; he looked like a kind of nerdy Joe College type always looking around smiling at people, sneaking peeks at the ladies but avoiding eye contact. Willie figured shit no skin off my ass, whatever floats G's boat. As long as he ain't sweatin me, he can let whoever kiss his ass, I don't give a granny goose shit.

Willie was cleaning up when he saw Lil G's Caddy pull up; he got out and walked to the door alone. "Young blood, young blood" Willie crowed, "Been a good month step into my office and let me pour you an early morning libation". What Willie didn't see was Lil G tripping open the dead-bolt lock on the door when he turned his back and headed for the office.

Willie sat down and reached into his desk drawer pulling out a large manila envelope stuffed with cash; "Just like I promised paid in full". Big Willie full of bravado said, "Now if you just slide my paperwork to me we can discuss taking our business to the next level, the sky is the limit young blood I got a ton of ideas that will make us both blow up big time". "Oh yeah about that" Lil G muttered, "First there's someone that would like to talk to you". A large ominous figure stepped into the doorway causing the outside light to silhouette his shape in a solar eclipse configuration. Big Willie attempted to focus his eyes in an attempt to filter out the Sunday morning sunlight that radiated around the huge Sasquatch like figure who filled up damn near every inch of the open doorway. The scene even unnerved Lil G who had instinctively moved silently toward the corner of the room making sure he was clear of the event-horizon formed by the massive black-hole in Big Willie Greene's office doorway. Ever so slowly the colossal figure progressed thru the door and towered inches from Willie's desk.

There stood none other than Mad Dog Max himself, all 6' 9" 325lbs of solid Sicilian muscle, the meanest most merciless shylock east of the Mississippi River. Most loan sharks had hired leg breakers to do their collection work but not Max, he actually loved making good on bad debts. When Willie fled Philly the Philadelphia District Attorney and those three ex-wives all figured they'd seen the last of Mr. Big Willie Greene; they all moved on to other endeavors. But that was not a part of Mad Max's DNA, as far as he was concerned no debt went uncollected and the juice on Willies' loan now had far surpassed payment in cash. His reputation was at stake; no one had ever stiffed Mad Dog Max for so much as a penny and lived to talk about it. A hard and harsh retribution would send a message loud and clear to anyone who even remotely entertained the idea of skipping out on Mad Dog. "How youse doing Willie" Max asked in that thick south Philly accent, as he pulled the sawed-off shotgun from underneath his coat.

"If you'll excuse me gentlemen" Lil G said, "It seems like you have some personal business to discuss", as he turned and headed for the front door carefully putting Big Willie Greene's deed and power of attorney in the breast pocket of his suit coat.

He smiled that sinister smile of his as he thought of the morning after Willie had made his proposal. Lil G had a cousin who lived in Philadelphia make inquiries as to the where-a-bouts of a Mad Dog Max, the local Philly shylock. It seemed that when Willie skipped town he was into Mad Dog for twenty large of unpaid gambling debts. G then hit the speed dial on his cell; the answer machine picked up. "Quincy Whittenberg, Architects and Construction, the office is closed please leave a message". "Q this G, the project is on you can start work on "Club West" in two weeks".

"Hey Tray, Smiley you two knuckleheads listening to me", Lil G yelled at his two deformed posse members. Tray and Smiley both turned around at the same time staring at Lil G, "Yeah boss we all ears" Smiley said. Bullshit G thought, those ears were burned off with damn near everything else; "I was saying the first thing we gotta do is eliminate the competition. All these freelance operators are a pain in the ass. I want to consolidate the distribution network to just one reliable supplier, that means everybody will have to deal exclusively with us and us alone. All the major players and small independents will have to come to "TLC" for product at our price and under our control". "But boss how do we get to all these guys; there must be five or six distributers in the L.A. area alone. Finding out just who the hell they are and where they hang is gonna take forever and a day". "Don't you worry about that" G said reaching for Big Spooky's portfolio, "Just get the boys ready for some work, I want everybody back here by seven". G poured himself a Hennessy and flipped open the black portfolio to a page that had not only pictures of every major drug dealer in Los Angeles, but a complete dossier on each including a breakdown of their operation, the territory which they controlled, security measures, the location of their stashes, and where they lived.

"Man Big Spooky did his homework" G laughed to himself. "With the information in this folder I'll be running this town in no time"; he then turned to the section in the back of the portfolio. There were the 8X10 color photos of Thelma, James and Paul; "After everybody's here and I brief them I have a special job for you two".

Chapter 12

THELMA CAN COOK

THELMA HAD SUGGESTED that they come over to her place where they could discuss the situation and try to formulate a plan over dinner. "Cool" said Paul "I'm starving like Marvin, I guess dead folks like us still get hungry. I couldn't eat that hospital slop, what's on the menu". "Oh I guess I could throw together something", Thelma said. "How about some smothered steak, macaroni and cheese, I have some left-over greens and you have to try my special Jabo Johnson Monkey Bread". "Oh hell yeah" screamed Paul, "Thel I'm down lets bounce". "Is that alright with you James are you hungry", asked Thelma. "Why yes I do believe I am, but I have a very delicate digestive system. Just what kind of salad greens will you serve and I am not sure if I will be able to handle a bakery item named after a primate".

As Paul put his head in his hands and moaned, Thelma said "Don't worry James I guarantee you'll enjoy it. Help Paul to your car and you guys follow me; I live over in Inglewood". "Inglewood" interjected James looking concerned; "Don't stress bro I'll protect you" Paul said, still shaking his head.

Paul pushed himself away from the table patting his stomach, "Damn Thelma girl you can burn. Those greens and that monkey bread was off the chain I'm stuffed. Yo James I bet you don't grub like this up in the hills" Paul continued, with a toothpick dangling out of his mouth bouncing back and forth like a conductor's baton. "Mmmmm" was the only response James could mutter with his mouth full of mac and cheese; he was working on his third helping. "Better slow down James" Thelma giggled, "You're not gonna have room for my Blackberry Cobbler". "Blackberry Clobber" Paul shouted, toothpick flying out of his mouth like a scud missile and exploding against the kitchen wall. "Hell Thelma don't waste no Blackberry Cobbler on homey, he ain't ready for that; you gotta break him in slowly". James stuffing another piece of monkey bread into his mouth never looked up.

Thelma just watched as James and Paul ate like two hyenas on the Serengeti, it made her feel good inside to see them enjoying themselves from the fruits of her labor.

It had been a long time since she had cooked for anyone other than herself. She had forgotten how much she enjoyed being in the kitchen. Her grandmother, Mama Lizzie as she was known had taught her how to navigate around the kitchen when she was a young girl living in Ruston, Louisiana. Mama Lizzie was undoubtedly the best cook in the parish and she passed on all her secrets and recipes to Thelma before she died at the age of one hundred and three.

Thelma remembered Lizzie saying, "Baby if you wanna be a good cook you have to put your foot in the pot, if you wanna be a great cook you gotta put your foot and a little of your heart and soul in there as well, then serve it up with love". Thelma's eyes were starting to swell with tears as she reminisced of her childhood.

She was born in Lake Charles, Louisiana the only child to Opal and Ervin Maddox. Her mother Opal had been a school teacher and her father Ervin a staff sergeant in the Marine Corps. Thelma was only five years old when her father was killed in Vietnam; he had been on one of the last helicopters evacuating refugees from the Saigon Embassy when it was shot down killing all on board. As young as she was, Thelma still remembered the change in her mother after her fathers' death. Her health steadily declined over the next few years, Opal finally passed due to complications from pneumonia. She died on Thelma's ninth birthday. Mama Lizzie used to tell Thelma that her mother died of a broken heart. "Your mother and father were so very much in love that she just couldn't go on without him", Lizzie explained. "The only thing that kept her going those years after his death was her devotion to you child", Lizzie further explained.

Mama Lizzie would tell Thelma that she inherited her mother's good sense and her father's toughness. Thelma did the best she could to live up to her parents expectations. She did well academically; and as far as taking care of herself, her fathers' tough resolve was ever present. Thelma did not back down from a fight, no matter who the adversary.

Once in high school Kathy Bellman, the principles daughter who had been jealous of Thelma since the third grade, started to spread rumors that Thelma's popularity was due only to the fact that she would put out to any boy who asked for it. Upon finding out the source of these rumors, Thelma confronted Kathy one day after school on the playground. "It's been brought to my attention that you been saying some very deceitful things about me", Thelma hissed at Kathy as she carefully sat her books down and began to remove her earrings.

Kathy seeing the look on Thelma's face knew immediately that she had royally fucked up. In her attempt to avoid the forthcoming beat-down, Kathy spun around on her axis and started to pull a Jesse Owens in the opposite direction. She was at full fight gallop when the basketball pole, which she didn't see made it's abrupt appearance.

Two missing front teeth and a black eye later, Kathy was telling her father how Thelma Mae Maddox had attacked her with a baseball bat because she had confronted her about some stolen earrings. "You degenerate thieving little bitch", Principle Bellman was yelling at Thelma as she sat across from him in his office. "How dare you attack my daughter with a baseball bat". "Sir I never" Thelma began, just as the principle reached across the desk and slapped Thelma as hard as he could. The blow knocked Thelma out of the chair and onto the floor drawing blood from the corner of her bottom lip. Thelma shaking loose the cobwebs and ignoring the singing tweety birds in her head stumbled to her feet. On the way up she grabbed Principle Bellman's Webster's Unabridged Dictionary which was sitting on the edge of his desk and let go with a mighty swing Hank Aaron would be proud of. The dictionary caught Principle Bellman dead center in the face.

As consequence would have it, the damage was two missing front teeth and a black eye. The only difference between Kathy and her father's injuries were which eye was blackened; daddy's left and daughter's right. And of course one was self-inflicted against a basketball pole; the other was the result of Thelma using Webster's Dictionary to show Principle Bellman her definition of the term Due Process. It was right after that incident Mama Lizzie decided that it might be a good idea if Thelma spent some time with her Aunt Sarah in Los Angeles.

After graduating from Thomas Jefferson High School located on 41st and Hooper Ave., not too far from Central Ave., Thelma enrolled at West Los Angeles Jr. College. She attended for one year before quitting and going to work full time at the post office. It was there she met and fell in love with Ronald Johnson, a good looking slick talking, ex-hustler from Inglewood.

Ronald was eight years her senior and had been working at the post office a couple of years before she got there. He had been involved in a few minor run-ins with the law during what he called his street days, but nothing serious enough to be kept from holding federal employment.

The first day Thelma laid eyes on Ronald she was immediately smitten. It was something about the way he carried himself that made her both giddy and excited. Thelma was anything but naïve; she had shaken that "hicks from the sticks" tag a long time ago and was Los Angeles street-wise as any born Angelino. She knew a player when she saw one and the fact that Ronald was undeniably a ladies man didn't really faze her. She had always been attracted to guys with that edge; she had often laughed at herself for being a sucker for "the bad boy image". Thelma and Ronald dated back and forth for a couple of years before he convinced her he was have to get serious and come up with a plan. Get yourselves together and join me in the living room". "Right behind you" Paul said, as he helped James to his feet. "Man you alright in my book" Paul said looking James square in the eye. "You have to forgive me; sometimes I put my mouth in gear while leaving my brain in neutral". James staring right back said, "I also must apologize I realize that I can come off as rather stiff and pompous at times, but my intentions are well meant". "I feel you, it's all good" Paul said. The whole kitchen scenario had somehow cemented a bond between the three; a kind of coronation of kinship and trust had formed. This was especially true of the relationship between Paul and James.

In a place far off and unseen, Gus began to smile.

Chapter 13

ELIMINATE THE COMPETITION

THELMA WAS SETTLING back down on the sofa when she noticed the breaking news icon on the television. "We interrupt this program to bring you the latest development in the multiple shootings that has taken place throughout the city". The news anchorwoman was saying that what we know so far is that three people in the Hollywood area were found shot to death execution style in the parking lot of a popular nightclub. In Inglewood, an entire family was found gun down in their home, in El Segundo two men were murdered in an underground garage, and a drive by shooting took the lives of eight people dining at a sidewalk café on Westwood Blvd. near the UCLA campus. Details are very sketchy at this time, but a police spokesperson did say that several of those involved were known drug dealers or were under investigation by law enforcement for various other crimes. They wouldn't say if these shootings were all gang or drug related, but they did ask the public to contact authorities if they had any information.

Just as Thelma was about to call for James and Paul, she turned around and saw them both standing in the doorway staring at the television. "My gracious" James said, "Do you think that G character has something to do with this". "Bet your sweet ass he did" Paul answered, "That little

There were red lights and emergency vehicles everywhere. Fire trucks and police cars blocked off the street. People were milling about behind yellow caution and crime scene tape that law enforcement uses to keep people out of the area while they conduct their investigations. "Thelma, help me out of the car" Paul ordered upon recognizing Del Roberts, the young teen who lived across the street from his mother. The youngster was standing wide-eyed in the crowd watching in amazement along with the rest of the neighborhood. "Hey Del" Paul hollered, scrambling out of the back seat of the Jaguar wincing as he banged his injured ankle against the curb. "Del what happened, what's going on".

"Paul somebody blew up your house, dude. Some terrorist or something drove up and fired one of those rocket things right through the front window. Mr. Crawford saw the whole thing; the cops are over at his place talking to him right now". "Dude just look at that", Del said excitingly pointing down the block to where the firefighters were putting out the last remnants of the smothering structure. Paul ignoring the pain in his right ankle broke through the crowd, breaking the crime scene tape, and rushed by the crowd control officers. He was almost at top speed when someone reached out and grabbed him by the arm.

"Mr. Logan I'm Detective Dave Marino, I saw you drive up and was on my way to speak to you". "Where's my family" Paul screamed, grabbing the detective by the lapels. "Calm down Mr. Logan, it seems no one was home. We were hoping that you could provide us with some information on the location of your mother and sisters". "No one was home, are you sure" Paul asked, releasing his grip from the detective's suit coat. "Yes we're sure. The house was empty; thank God no one was injured. Who are those folks that drove up with you" Marino continued, looking suspiciously at James and Thelma who were making their way through the crowd. "They're friends of mine", Paul answered just as James and Thelma approached. "This is Thelma Johnson and James Pettigrew".

Thelma ignoring the police detective asked, "Paul is your family alright". "They weren't home but nobody's heard from them", he answered. Paul was starting to get anxious again. "I'll tell you what; my partner is interviewing your mother's neighbor, a Mr. Ricky Crawford over at his place. Let's all go over there where we can have some privacy before the media descends on us like locust. Mr. Pettigrew I'll give your car keys to one of the officers and have them drive your automobile up to Mr. Crawford's house". As they entered the living room, Detective John Holloway was just finishing up with Mr. Crawford's declaration.

"Now make sure I got this right," the detective was saying. "You were just coming back from taking your dog for her walk, when you noticed a tan colored van pull up in front of Mrs. Logan's house. Then two individuals emerged with what looked like a shoulder held rocket launcher and fired it through the front window". "That's correct" answered the neighbor. "That is exactly what happened, they then jumped back in the van and tore ass down the street, kinda shook me up and scared the hell out of Andie". "Who", asked the detective. "Andie my dog, she's an American Cocker Spaniel, smart as a whip but a little high strung. Can't say that I blame her, I haven't seen anything like that since Korea. I was at the 'Chosin Reservoir' you know; froze my ass off fighting those commie bastards, lost a lot of good Marines over that frozen piece of landscape".

"Yes sir, but can you recall anything else about the two individuals", asked Holloway. "Only that they were the two ugliest ass-holes I've ever laid eyes on", answered Mr. Crawford.

"After they fired that thing off and the house caught fire, I got a glimpse of both their faces". "Yeah go on" urged the detective, "What did they look like"? "The butt-ugly twins; like I said I was a Marine and saw a lot of combat in Korea; I saw scores of bodies that had been killed and burned by napalm. And both those fellows looked like they had gone a couple of rounds with a flame-thrower. But nobody could have been roasted and toasted that bad and survived, so I'd have to say they were born that way and then suffered a major beating from the same ugly stick".

"Yes sir", interjected Detective Marino. "Besides being butt-ugly, could you tell what nationality they were; black, white, Hispanic". "Hell your guess is as good as mine", Mr. Crawford answered. "I'd have to say they were a charcoal briquette, ash type of color. You have to pick what nationality that would be".

As the two police officers looked at each other trying to figure out what to say next, Paul approached. "Mr. Crawford do you remember me, I'm Lucy's son". "Sure I know who you are; you signed with the Clippers, now that took guts". I'm just funning with you son", the old man said. "Your mother said you were going to turn that team around, she's very proud of you young man". "Thank you Mr. Crawford, do you have any idea where my mother and sisters are". "Sorry son, I haven't seen them since that limo picked them up". "What limo", both the detectives said simultaneously. "The one that rolled up about noon, it was one of those long stretched out jobs, pearly white if I recall correctly.

At that moment Paul's cell phone rang. "Hi honey I just got your message, are you alright". "Mama where are you, are you ok, where's Pam and Karen". "Slow down Paul", Lucy said. "You're scaring me, what's wrong". Paul regaining some composure said. "Sorry mama I was just a little worried about you and the girls". "Why, we're just fine, it's so beautiful and peaceful here. And everyone's treating us like royalty; the girls are having the time of their lives". Paul was utterly perplexed, but he didn't want to let on to Lucy that he had no idea what she was talking about. "That's good mama, I just wanted to make sure you guys got to . . . ; what's the name of the place again". "La Costa silly, this resort is like Karen says the bomb".

"They cater to your every need; we've already had a mud bath, a Swedish massage, a manicure and a pedicure. Tomorrow morning we get golf lessons, another beauty treatment, and at sunset a horseback ride through the desert. And that limo driver Gus was the best. He sang songs and told jokes the whole drive down here. He told us you wanted us to be surprised, to just pack for the weekend and be prepared to live the life. I didn't want to go at first because of your accident, but Gus said you were fine and wanted us to relax while you recuperated. He was very convincing and so darn nice I couldn't refuse". "You are so right mama that Gus is the best and I am just fine. Everything is alright, there was a small fire at the house, nothing to worry about, you guys have fun and I'll see you on Monday". "A fire" Lucy started. "No big deal mama, really I'll handle it", Paul said. "Enjoy yourself and tell the girls their big brother says hi; I love you mama". "I love you to baby".

James was driving east on Sunset Blvd. "I think you really upset those detectives not telling them where your mother was, but I believe that was the wise thing to do". "I agree", said Thelma. "I don't think we have to worry about them anymore, something tells me they will be safe until this thing is over". Paul stretched out in the back seat, nodded in agreement. "Old Gus sure came through".

Chapter 14

BIG SPOOKY DON'T PLAY

LIL G WAS leaning back in the oversize black leather desk chair that Willie Greene had loved so much; it was one the few items that belonged to Willie that G had decided to keep. He kept the chair along with the many framed and autographed photographs of the celebrities who had visited Willie's barbershop back in Philly. His favorite was the one of Muhammad Ali seating in the barber chair with the barber's cape clipped around his neck. Ali was posing with that playful menacing scowl of his, biting his bottom lip, his right fist raised at Willie. He had signed the photo, "Next time I come to Philly, if you make me wait, I'll beat you Silly", signed "The Champ". Lil G was sipping on a snifter of Hennessy and staring at the photo hanging on the wall directly in front of his desk when Tray and Smiley walked thru the back door.

"How'd it go, any problems with that surplus rocket launcher". "No problem", answered Tray. "We went Rambo Commando on that bitch. "Yeah, we lit her ass up", chimed in Smiley. "You should've seen that house go up; boom, bang, and boom again, shit was flying everywhere". Tray and Smiley were giggling like two schoolgirls, they were high-fiving each other as if they had just scored the winning touchdown in the Super Bowl.

"Shut up", Lil G hollered as he noticed the Breaking News icon on the wall unit television. "There has been an explosion at a home in the Pacific Palisades area of West Los Angeles, early reports indicate unknown assailants may have deliberately caused the explosion, but that has not been confirmed at this time. It has however been confirmed by authorities that there were no causalities. We do not know if this latest development has any connection to the previous murders that has taken place thru out the city. Again there has been an explosion at a home in Pacific Palisades, no report of injuries . . ."

Lil G was up on his feet leaning over the desk screaming at Tray and Smiley. "You two inept, stupid, dumb asses hear that; no injuries, no casualties, what the hell". "But boss", Smiley and Tray said at the same time. "We fired right thru the front window". "Did you check to see if anyone was at home first", G asked eyes glaring, shaking his head and grinding his teeth. Tray and Smiley looking at each other, simultaneously whispered. "You were supposed to check; no asshole you were supposed to check". Lil G was fit to be tied, just as he was trying to figure out what to do next, a chilling numbing cold descended on the room.

All sound ceased to exist; the air became thick and gave off a static discharge that caused any metal surface in the office to glow in an eerie amber color. The ominous environment had the hairs on the back of Lil G's neck doing the tingle boogie as a feeling of dread and horror slowly crept up his spine. He slowly turned around not knowing what to expect. There stood the portentous shadowlike tall figure he called Big Spooky, hovering directly behind him.

"Failure will not be tolerated", rang crystal clear in Lil G's head. **"Choose who will be punished"**, as the tall aberration pointed his long robe covered arm at Tray and Smiley. **"Choose who will suffer the fate of failure"** "What do you mean", mentally expressed Lil G. "Choose who for what". **"Choose one of these two, one must suffer the fate"**, came the reply. Lil G looked at Tray and Smiley who were both staring wide-eyed and petrified. Lil G again forgetting about replying mentally said very loudly. "Hey man these two are my homeboys, we came up together, we been boys from way back, cut'em some slack". **"Choose or suffer the fate yourself"**, came the reply. **"Now"**

Chapter 15

L. Z. STEADY ON THE CASE

INGLEWOOD DETECTIVE L.Z. (Andy) Anderson's thoughts were the same as every other homicide police officer in the greater Los Angeles area; he was trying to figure out what the hell was going on with all these murders. Seventeen shootings taking place almost simultaneously spread out from Hollywood to El Segundo. That included a family of four over on Cedar and Nectarine. "Shit that's just three blocks from the station", L.Z. muttered to himself. "A whole family gun down in their own home and nobody saw dick. Hell, you don't have to be a genius to know these killings have to be drug related", L.Z. surmised loudly. "Somebody is making a major move and they are not taking any prisoners. If all these department leaders would pull their heads out of their collective asses long enough to take a fresh breath, they would organize a multi-agency effort of cooperation to pool resources and share information. To hell with waiting for an official request to come through channels; Marino over at LAPD Westside owes me a favor or two. I think I'll call one in", L.Z. thought to himself as he reached for the phone.

"Hey Big Wave Dave, you working hard or hardly working", L.Z. said. "L.Z. long time, no hear from", answered Detective Dave Marino. "How are Mary and the kids"? "They're just fine Dave and Celeste, she still putting up with your sorry ass". "You know L.Z., love must be blind; Celeste is still hanging in there". "Love my ass; you're just like me working all the time, we're never home long enough to get on our wives nerves. Just drop off the paycheck, change clothes, grab a bite, and back on the street. "You got that right", Marino shot back laughing. "Let me guess, you're sucking on a large Starbucks and trying to get a grip on these shootings; how am I doing".

"You hit the nail on the head buddy. You know I've got to get my coffee fix on, and I'd like to hear your spin on all this mayhem". "I'd have to say someone's making a bold move on the drug scene", answered Marino. "And when I say bold, that's with a capital B. I mean these aren't low level dealers getting their heads handed in.

These guys are at the top of the food chain; I understand that those guys that got hit in Westwood were number one with a bullet on the DEA's all-star team. Allegedly they were the last direct link between what's left of the Columbia Cartel and the west coast. Last year they were responsible for over fifty percent of all the cocaine west of the Rockies. A buddy of mine with the DEA said they were within a gnat's fart of indicting half that bunch".

"Now the Feds are going ape-shit trying to figure out the master-mind behind all this; I mean they don't have a single blip on their radar. Personally, I think it's a lot bigger than some new sheriff in town". "What do you mean", asked L.Z. "I mean think about it, here you have all the heavyweight drug king-pins being taken out as easy as you please; and all within a day and a half. Come on L.Z. these guys aren't amateurs, most of them have better security than the president and neither the Feds nor us knew where half of them were before two days ago. Just imagine the kind of intel, surveillance, and coordination that it would take to pull off something like that."

"Dave are you trying to tell me this could be some sort of government conspiracy or terrorist plot against drug dealers", L.Z. laughed. "No L.Z. I'm not saying that, I'm just saying that there is a lot of strange shit going on lately. Hell I just pulled a case where somebody used one of those hand-held rocket launchers to blow up this basketball player mothers'

Chapter 16

THE PETTIGREW ESTATE

AFTER THE ENCOUNTER with the two detectives at Mr. Crawford's house, James suggested they make the short drive over to his family's estate up in Bel-Air to regroup. Big James Sr. had moved the family into the exclusive Bel-Air section above Beverly Hills five years earlier. He had personally scouted the entire Bel-Air area to find a home which would provide not only comfort, but security and privacy for the family. He settled on the estate owned by one of Hollywood's major studio executives. And even though the movie mogul had no inclination to sale; Big James made him an offer too generous to turn down. He then spent an additional one million dollars to renovate the property to his specific specifications.

As young James, Thelma, and Paul pulled up to the security guard kiosk, a uniformed security officer approached. In one hand he held a clipboard; the other hand was resting Wyatt Earp style on the butt of his holstered firearm. Paul and Thelma were looking around as though they had just entered the Magic Kingdom at Disney World. "Damn", Thelma gasped. "That guard house is as large as my whole duplex". "No shit", chuckled Paul. "Hey James that security dude is checking us out like we the Dillinger Gang or something, I hope you got some ID on you, bro". "Not to worry you two", smiled James.

"Hello William", James said as he extended his hand to the approaching guard. "Oh Mr. Pettigrew, I'm sorry sir I didn't recognize you". "It's quite alright William; it's been awhile since I've been to the estate, anyone home". "No sir, I believe your father is out of town on business, but you're your grandfather is due back this evening from Las Vegas. The gardener just left about an hour ago, the house is completely empty. Is there anything I can do for you sir". "No thank you William, but we may be ordering out a bit later, I'll let you know".

Thelma looking in the back seat at Paul said. "No Dillinger Gang here stretch, we the James Gang".

As James pulled the Jaguar into the long circular driveway, the enormity of the three story structure was not lost on Paul and Thelma. "Jeez this place is humongous".

"Is this a house or a hotel", asked Paul. "Grandfather said it was just large enough to keep the family under one roof and still provide adequate space for everyone's privacy, especially his. The north wing is where he spends most of his time and is generally off limits to anyone without permission". "Sounds a little cloak and dagger", Thelma said. "Just what does your grandfather do"?

"Oh he is a very important and influential figure in the Southern California business and political arena", James answered with swelling pride. "He came to Los Angeles right after World War II, started a small restaurant, then ventured into real estate and other business endeavors". "Well I ain't mad at him", said Paul. "Judging by the size of this crib, homey got paid big time. Tell gramps if he's looking for a partner, I'm down. So big money, who else stays here besides your grandpop and your father". "Well right now, it's pretty much just the two of them. My aunts come and go periodically, depending on if they're between husbands, but that's another story", James said. Paul and Thelma both thought maybe it would be wise to let that one go.

"What about you", Thelma asked. "The place ain't big enough for the three of you", she said facetiously. "It's not that at all", James said smiling. I just prefer to go it alone and make my own way. I'd like to build my own template and become successful the way my grandfather did; on my own terms. I just hope I can become half the man he is. I've looked up to him my entire life and pray that I have inherited some of his grit and determination. "I wouldn't worry", Thelma said. "You'll be just fine".

Just as James, Thelma, and Paul were getting comfortable in the large family room situated in the south wing, Lil G was stuffing a bloody shirt and pants in the bed of the gray pick-up truck between the lawnmower and a leaf blower. When he had settled in the back seat of the Escalade, he caressed Big Spooks' portfolio and flipped open his cell phone.

Chapter 17

THE JIG IS UP

"GUYS WE HAVE to bust a move on G's ass before he comes after us again", Paul was saying. All of a sudden James' cell phone rang. "Yo, Madison Ave. you know who I am". James recognized the voice from the earlier confrontation at Thelma's. "Yes I certainly know to whom I'm conversing with. You're the cowardly miscreant that terrorizes defenseless women and children". I can't imagine a lower form of human excrement than one who would prey on the helpless."

"Yeah, yeah shouted G, whatever. I told you what would happen if you three interfered in my business, that white boy got lucky, but guess what Mr. Fancy Ass; your luck ran out or should I say your granddaddy's luck just ran out". The expression on James' face sent ice shivers thru both Thelma and Paul who were watching intently; they knew he was talking with the nefarious young gangster. "What about my grandfather, what have you done", shouted James. "Me, I ain't done shit, it's what the great Big James Pettigrew Sr. has been doing all these years. Turns out the old man is quite a playa, I kind of admire the old dude it seems like we have a lot in common".

"You lying little degenerate, what possibly you and my grandfather could have in common he's dedicated his entire life to rid the stench that you and your kind inflict on our people. How dare you have the unmitigated gall to suggest that my grandfather would have anything even remotely to do with the likes of you." Paul and Thelma were now extremely concerned James was trembling, the color had faded from his face, and he was screaming into the mouthpiece of his cell phone. Thelma shouted, "James what's going on, what's that bastard saying, where's your grandfather". "Tell that bitch to shut the fuck up", Lil G snapped at James, "I'll get around to her soon enough. And as far as old grandpa is concerned, why don't the three of you just stroll over to his office. I left a little something, something for old playa, playa". "What do you mean you left something, my grandfather is not interested in anything that has to do with you", James started to say. "Not quite true", G shot back, "Why don't you let old pops be the judge of that. And oh yeah, be careful not to trip over that lump in the hallway".

James and Thelma were sprinting to the north wing of the estate with Paul limping not far behind. They raced thru the vestibule that separated the two wings of the large mansion and started down the long corridor of the north wing that led to the private office where James Sr. spent the majority of his time. Thelma was about ten feet behind James and maybe ten to twelve feet ahead of Paul. As she entered the north wing corridor she couldn't help but notice the photos that lined both walls of the long hallway; there were pictures she surmised of the Pettigrew family arranged in chronological order of each generation. There were baby pictures that seemed to progress thru puberty ending which each member posing for their college portrait. She didn't recognize anyone until she passed James' high school graduation cap and gown portrait. He looked so studious and proud she thought to herself, eager to carry on the proud tradition of the Pettigrew legacy. She then focused in on the large portrait which hung on the wall where the corridor elbowed into the hallway leading to Big James's office. Thelma thought the portrait looked like one of those she had seen on television or at the movies. It was like one that adorned the wall in some European castle or hung on display in a museum. There was big James Sr. himself, the patriarch of the Pettigrew Clan standing proudly in front of the mansion. He was dressed to the nines in formal attire which included tails, a cravat, spats, and a cane topped with a large diamond shaped handle. The man looked like royalty. It appeared to be one of those self-indulgent portraits like George Washington sitting on his horse overlooking his troops or Napoleon on some hilltop surveying he battlefield. Then it hit her; he reminded her of the actor George C. Scott portraying General George Patton standing in front of that large American flag at the beginning of that movie. For some reason that she couldn't rationalize to herself at that particular moment; she had an immediate distain for Big James Pettigrew Sr.

"Oh my God, oh no", James screamed from around the corner of the hallway shaking Thelma from her fixation on the large portrait. Paul bringing up the rear yelled, "What's up, what's going on bro". As Thelma's eyes focused in the low light down the hallway, she saw James standing over what appeared to be someone slumped on the floor. James was leaning with his back against the wall, both hands covering his mouth staring down in disbelief at the slumped figure.

Paul who had finally caught up with Thelma yelled, "Oh shit, who's that, yo James" he yelled louder, "WHO'S THAT". "It's Sam our gardener" James answered, "How could someone have done this".

Sam was slumped on the floor in a semi sitting position leaning against the wall in a blood soaked T-shirt that one could only guess had once been white; his throat had been cut from ear to ear. Thelma and Paul approaching had difficulty keeping their footing wading through the semi-dried blood which had pooled around the body on the hardwood floor. Thelma found herself speechless and getting nauseated as she stared down at the deceased gardener who lay back against the wall, legs spread wide apart. His eyes were open staring blankly up at James as though asking, "What the fuck".

The door at the end of the hallway which led to big James' office was slightly ajar; the light which oozed around the edge of the door and down the darken hallway exacerbated an already macabre and eerie sensation among the trio. Almost simultaneously the three of them stared toward

James with trembling hands slowly opened the folder which Lil G had left. Inside were a legal size manila envelope and some old newspaper articles. The first article detailed the gangland murder of some criminal named Ben Buford. Buford was reportedly the head of black organized crime in the late 40's and early 50's in Los Angeles, as James read out loud for Thelma and Paul, the article went on to say Buford was under investigation for drug trafficking among other crimes. Just days before he was to be indicted by the Los Angeles Grand Jury; he was found murdered behind the wheel of his car in the parking lot of Club Alabam, a popular jazz club on Central Ave. He had been stabbed to death with an ice pick. The next article was that of a major drug seizure in a warehouse located on 118th and Avalon, the Feds had raided the warehouse on a tip from an informant. Seized were more than fifty pounds of heroin and two hundred pounds of marijuana hidden under a tarp along the warehouse wall. The article had a grainy and faded photo of police and federal agents pointing to the stack of the seized drugs. There was something disturbing to James as he looked at the photo, he couldn't figure out why the picture was causing his stomach to tie up in a granny knot, suppressing the uneasy feeling he read on.

Arrested on site were two known criminals who had ties to Ben Buford and his organization, the article also went on to say that before these two gangsters could provide any pertinent information to the federal authorities they both were killed in an auto accident on the very day they made bail. The car they were driving was found at the bottom of a ravine off Mulholland Dr. overlooking West Hollywood. James who had started to sweat profusely took a deep breath and reached for the manila envelope. He pulled out an 8"x10" black and white photo and what appeared to be two old faded out bail bond certificates. The bail bond certificates were from 'The James Pettigrew Bail Bond Service'; the one which big James had started back in 1951 after picking up a couple of two story office buildings on Western Ave. in one of his real estate ventures.

The names on the certificates matched those of the two arrestees from the warehouse drug bust mentioned in the article.

The 8'x10' photo was almost identical as the one shown in the newspaper article, only larger and much clearer. It showed in detail not only the law enforcement officers and the drugs, but also the decorum of the warehouse itself. The wall behind the drug seizure was adorned with a collection of fight posters, the most prominent being the 1938 Joe Louis vs. Max Schemling title fight. James suddenly realized why the photograph was so familiar and where he had seen it before. "Thelma bring me that photo album from the top shelf on the middle bookcase", James commanded pointing across the room. When Thelma handed him the photo album, he flipped about half way thru stopping at an 8"x10" glossy black and white. The picture was of a birthday party thrown for James Sr. by some of his friends and business associates. The picture showed a long fancy decorated table with a large birthday cake situated in the middle. There was a banner stretched end to end on the front of the tablecloth which read 'Happy Birthday James P. The King of Central Ave.' there was balloons and ribbons adorning the wall behind the table just above the boxing posters. James remembered thumbing thru the album years ago when exploring his grandfather's office while he was out town on business. The poster of Joe Louis had caught his eye because his history class was discussing the period leading up to World War II and how Joe Louis defeating Germany's Max Schmeling and Jesse Owens success at the 1936 Olympics in Germany had embarrassed Adolph Hitler. There was no doubt; this was the same warehouse where the drugs seizure had taken place.

Standing behind the birthday cake in the photo was a much younger James Pettigrew Sr. shaking hands with a dapper dressed man smoking a long fat cigar. There were about twelve men and women sitting along the table; someone had written in names on the photograph above each person sitting at the table. Written above the man shaking hands with James Sr. was the name Ben Buford.

"All this cannot be true", James said. "This is some kind of trick by this G character to involve my grandfather for some reason. He's doing this to get at us, at me, remember what Gus said; to be aware of Lil G's cunning wickedness". Thelma and Paul glanced at each other, somehow they knew that this wasn't a trick; James' grandfather had a sinister side and they both knew it.

"Yo James" Paul said, "Play the tape". James nervously hit the play button. "Hey assholes, the jig is up. As you can see I ain't the only bad guy in town", Lil G was chuckling over the cassette tape. "It seems old Big Game James is on a level I'm trying to reach, a real master criminal type. Old pops is the Michael Jordan of gangsters, the original OG. That little evidence I left you is just the tip of the iceberg. The old man has been wheeling and dealing since the late forties. And it looks like he didn't take any prisoners if someone got in his way. The old dude has been putting in work for a long time. I got all the proof Five-O will need to tie the old man into drug trafficking, extortion, bribery and the murders of a zillion motherfuckers including Ben Buford and those two from his crew that mysteriously drove off the cliff after being bailed out. Now that I have your undivided attention this is what I want; you tell the old man he is to turn me onto all his South American suppliers, that includes the Juarez Cartel in Bogotá. I also want access to his political and military contacts in Mexico. He doesn't have to worry about the distribution network here; as you probably already know I've taken care of that little problem. All he has to do is convince those greedy ass Columbians that he is transitioning the entire west coast operation over to me. He can tell them he has cancer, he's getting too old, he found Jesus, whatever I don't care. Just make sure those South Americans dick-heads realize that; I'm the man from now on. They deal with me or they don't deal at all.

I don't give a rat's ass how the old prune gets it done, but I expect his answer when I call back. Otherwise Mike Wallace and the 60 minute television crew will be knocking on the door asking a lot of hard questions. Can you guys envision that scenario on the six o'clock news, the Feds hauling the old man away in handcuffs along with your father and your aunts. Yeah that's right sweet pea, your pops and those two gold digging conniving aunts of yours knew exactly what was going down. But hey, I guess when you get used to the good life one has a tendency to look the other way; can't really blame them. I mean that is a real nice crib, but now it's my turn. It's time for me to pull my own George Jefferson and move on up. Tell the old bastard I'll be in contact. Oh yeah, also tell him he better clean up my handy work in the hallway there, we can't have dead gardeners laying around all over the place; it makes for bad business, not to mention tripping hazards". The tape ended with Lil G cackling that sinister laugh of his.

James leaned back in the chair and just stared blankly at the cassette player. Then in tornado fashion, a gambit of mixed emotions began to swirl around in his head. As each emotion fought to become the most dominate, it reflected itself in James' facial expressions. First came the look of shock and disbelief, he opened his mouth to say something but no sound emerged. If any of this was true then his whole life had been a sham, he had grown up in a made up environment of lies and subterfuge.

Everything that he was, everything that he had accomplished had come at the expense of those who had suffered under a criminal regime of drugs, mayhem, and murder. And then that look of disappointment and shame as the tears began to form around the corners of both eyes. How many times had his grandfather extolled the virtues of hard work and perseverance; those attributes along with education were the keys to success. Big James had preached that concept for as long as young James III could remember. Hell, just a couple of hours ago he had severely chastised Paul with that same sermon. The tears began to flow more freely; he couldn't even look in Paul's direction. And finally the anger which steamed from the tears and opened the adrenaline floodgates caused James to spring to his feet knocking over the chair he was sitting in.

He then pounded the desk with his fist hard enough to send the cassette player and desk lamp on a low trajectory to the floor. "That hypocritical old bastard" James screamed, causing Thelma and Paul to simultaneously jump backward and stare wide-eyed at the floored cassette player and desk lamp, then at James, then at each other. "Take it easy bro" Paul said as he attempted to grab James by the arm and guide him back to

overcoat. As they turned the corner at the end of the hallway, Big James could see the blanket covering something on the floor just outside his office. As they got closer he could make out the semi-dried blood on the floor, automatically his grip tightened in his overcoat pocket. He bent over and slowly pulled the blanket back revealing Sam's lifeless body staring up at the two of them. That previous "What the fuck" look now seemed to be saying, "Yeah and fuck you to asshole". "My God it's Sam" big James said. "Sonny who did this". "By all intent and purpose you did" answered young James as he walked thru the office door.

James sat and watched as his grandfather read thru the articles and listened to the tape that Lil G had left. He studied the older mans' face for some sign of emotional content, but big James sat there emotionless as he stolidly listened to Lil G's recorded demands. He then pulled out his cell phone and gave instructions to whoever answered to have a cleanup crew come over immediately. Then he phoned William at the gate and told him that some maintenance people were on the way to let them enter. Finally he looked up at the younger Pettigrew and asked, "Sonny who is this guy and just how you and those friends of yours are involved". "Just one minute", young James shouted. "I do believe I'm the one that is entitled to some answers here. Please tell me there is a viable explanation to all this, please tell me there has been some terrible mistake, that you are no way involved in this lunacy".

Big James stared at his grandson with a look that young James had never seen before; it was as though his whole persona metamorphosed into a character completely foreign to James. He leaned back in the large desk chair and reached into one of the drawers that contained the humidor which housed his favorite Cuban Cigars. Big James never took his eyes off his grandson as he snipped the end of the expensive Cuban with a diamond studded cigar clipper. He fired up the stogie and took a long slow drag, then proceeded to blow a large smoke ring that seemed to take on a life of its own. The hazy cigar smoke ring filtered by the light of the Tiffany Desk

Lamp floated across the desk toward young James and appeared to hover inches from his face before it dissipated into nothingness.

It was at that point James knew that everything Lil G had said was true. The aura projected by the elder Pettigrew penetrated young James to the core, it was all true. It was at that point that the respect and admiration James had felt for his grandfather emulated that smoke ring and also dissipated into nothingness.

"Ok Sonny" the old man said coolly as he blew another smoke ring. "I guess it's about time we both came to Jesus. So wipe that holier than thou look off your face and hear me out before you pass judgment". The old man settled back in the oversize desk chair and began to tell his story.

"After the war I came to California with nothing except my muster out pay and what the army taught me about being a cook. But I had a plan. I took my meager savings and the experience the army gave me and planned to carve out a good life for my family and myself. Both my grandfather and father worked themselves to death sharecropping in Mississippi that was not going to be my destiny. I worked my ass off to get started on Central Ave. You have no idea how difficult it was for a black man just to get a decent job in those days, let alone start his own business. You didn't just waltz into the local bank and apply for a small business loan, especially when you didn't have a pot to piss in or a window to throw it out of. So yes, I approached a couple of the areas' underworld figures to assist me with my financial problems".

"Now wait a minute" the younger James interrupted. "How does one go from borrowing money from a loan shark to becoming a major drug dealer with ties to the Columbia Cartel, how can you justify . . ." "Shut the hell up" the senior Pettigrew yelled at James. "You have no idea the circumstances I had to deal with. You've been cuddled and catered to your whole life, everything handed to you on a silver platter. You, your father, and both your aunts have had every advantage in life because of my efforts, the difference between you and them is; they have the good sense not to question their good fortune. Sonny my boy, you ought to buy a dog and cat and name them 'Common and Sense', so you'll have some". He then relit his stogie which had gone out and continued to tell young James how he got started on Central Ave.

Young James had made up his mind to bite his tongue and to listen without interruption; he sensed that he was hearing a story never told to anyone, he also sensed that the old man was unloading a great burden that he had been carrying all these years . . .

Chapter 19

LIFE ON THE AVENUE

THE YEAR WAS 1946; it had been almost a year since President Truman had given the go ahead to drop the two Atomic Bombs on Japan, thus putting an official end to World War II.

James Pettigrew had come to Los Angeles after mustering out of the army on advice from Lonniel Golston, an army buddy. He was twenty one years old, still in one piece with all his mental faculties and he had $1500 in his pockets. The war experience had not been too bad on James, after boot camp it was discovered that he had worked as a fry cook in Tupelo, Mississippi so he was assigned to the camp mess hall. While the rest of his company shipped out to Fort Hood, Texas to begin training as combat tank crews, James remained in Mississippi. Years later he would often wonder how he would have fared in combat. The black soldiers who trained at Fort Hood eventually went on to distinguish themselves as the 761st Tank Battalion, a highly decorated all-black combat unit in the European Campaign. James would correspond with buddies in the unit that kept him updated on their exploits. General George Patton himself had said they were one of the best fighting units in Europe. James wondered how much his life would have turned out different if he had gone overseas with the 761st

Even though James spent the entire war years in the states, he did manage to promote to the rank of sergeant based on his culinary and

of the blues, swing, and the big band influence. When Dizzy Gillespie and Charlie Parker showed up and introduced Be-Bop, true jazz aficionados couldn't stay away. The street was almost always bumper-to-bumper with streetcars and fancy automobiles that ferried a diverse clientele from every walk of life down to the avenue. Everyone clamored to experience this wide range of music that was the West Coast Jazz Scene.

The first week left James in total awe of the hustle and bustle that was taking place all around him; after all he really was a country boy fresh from the south. His only worldly experiences had been the regime of the military and listening to stories of big city life from his army buddies from New York, Chicago, Kansas City, and Los Angeles. And even though army buddy Lonniel had told him about the controlled mayhem that was life on the avenue; James was still mesmerized by the dapperly dressed black men and the beautiful women on their arms. He was even more amazed by the Zoot suited Mexicans and by the white men who showed up in black-tie and tails escorting movie starlet looking ladies dressed to the nines, all converging on Central Ave. looking for a good time.

James to say the least was a quick study, by week two he fit right in. He had shaken the country dust and the army reveille from behind his ears, purchased himself a couple of those dapper looking suits, learned to talk the talk, and strutted up and down the avenue like a veteran. He would pop in and out of the jazz clubs at night treating himself to performances by the likes of Teddy Edwards, Art Tatum, and Johnny Otis just to name a few. And he became friendly with many of the doormen working the clubs; these guys were the best source of information on the boulevard. A good doorman worth his salt had the low-down on everything and everybody. They also knew how to provide for the different clientele who requested anything from dollars to doughnuts. They could tell you depending on your preference; where the best places for sexual favors could be had, or what boosters had what merchandise available for the five-fingered discount, they could guide you to all the gambling dens and local loan sharks, or even who to approach if you wanted somebody to mysteriously disappear.

But it was a doorman named Clyde Price who worked a couple of the smaller clubs on the boulevard that James became particularly close to once it was discovered that they both had come from Tupelo. Clyde was called the 'Maestro' because he wore one of those marching band uniforms complete with gold shoulder epaulettes, a navy captains' cap, and carried a band conductors baton. He twirled and brandished that baton with such flair and pizzazz, that it never failed to gain the attention of the patrons who strolled along the avenue looking for entertainment.

Clyde was the person who introduced James to Ben Buford.

Chapter 20

BIG BEN BUFORD

BIG BEN BUFORD was an extremely intelligent, forty-five year old black man, who was always impeccably dressed. Physically he was an imposing figure that stood over six feet tall and weighed in at approximately two hundred and fifty pounds. He was completely bald with no hair showing anywhere including eyebrows, mustache, or beard. The absence of any hair made his dark skin seemed to shine and glisten with a sheen that would cause one to do a double take if he walked by. He had a broad and infectious smile that made you feel at ease in his presence; that was until that smile faded and he stared at you with piercing jet black eyes that had just the opposite effect. It was an unnerving glance that screamed bad intentions and made you frantically comb through your brain for something to say or do that would bring back that broad smile. Being such an imposing figure in stature was a direct contradiction when he spoke. His voice was soft and melodic with a slight Jamaican accent.

He had come to Los Angeles from Harlem, New York just before the war, rumor had it that he had been sent out west on orders from the east coast crime syndicate to organize their interest in Southern California. Rather this was true or just another rumor out of control didn't matter, everyone knew that Big Ben Buford operated outside of the law and was not a man to be trifled with.

Ben running into Clyde told him that he was throwing a big dinner party at his place and was looking for someone who knew their way around the kitchen to cater the event. His wife who usually handled such things was back east visiting a sick relative. Ben slipped a twenty dollar bill into Clyde's jacket pocket and said that this gathering was very important and that he needed someone that would help him make an impression. "I don't want to be embarrassed, get my drift Clyde" Ben said staring at Clyde with those piercing eyes. "Yes sir Mr. Buford I know just the guy, he's new in town and staying over at the Dunbar. They say he can make a rhinoceros ass taste like a New York T-Bone, I'll send him right over you won't be disappointed". "For your sake I better not be" Ben Buford said as he tossed another sawbuck at Clyde.

"Brother", Clyde said to James, "You better know how to burn like the devil himself. I mean you have to play a symphony with those pots and pans, or it's both our asses. If you fuck up on this dinner party, it's going to be us on the menu at the next one". James just smiled; he considered this an opportunity to impress one of the area big-wigs. He knew if he could get on the good side of Big Ben Buford, it could lead to his goal of establishing his own reputation in the community.

The dinner party was a big success; everyone just raved about the food and begged Ben to invite them back for dinner in the future. A few of the guest were even caught sneaking into the kitchen slipping James their business cards and making job offers to James behind Ben's back. After everyone had left, Ben offered James his first Cuban cigar as they sat and talked; they immediately hit it off.

"How would you like to come and work for me", Ben asked. "Mr. Buford no disrespect, but I came to California to start my own business, I want to open my own restaurant and be my own boss". Buford leaned back and blew a big smoke ring. "I understand and respect that" he said, "And by the way, call me Ben. I like the way you think, it's refreshing to see a young man that knows what he wants out of life. Suppose I can come up with something that would be mutually profitable for both of us". James was indeed intrigued by what Ben Buford was saying. "Would you be interested in an investment to get you started", Ben asked. "I think I would be very much interested Mr. Buford, oh excuse me, Ben. What kind of investment are we talking about". "Well you say you want to open your own eatery", Ben said. "That's all well and good, but you have to consider other factors besides being a good cook. There are management skills, which you undoubtedly gained in the army, the financial aspect, which is where I come in. But the most important factor in the restaurant business is location. You have to establish yourself where the people are. Again this is where I can be of great assistance. Do you know that little delicatessen across the street from the Dunbar".

"You mean the place run by that little old guy and his daughter, 'Bernie's' I think it's called", answered James. "Yeah that's the one" continued Ben, "Bernie Herzog, that little Jew bastard has been a thorn in my ass for too long". "That little old man, how's that", James asked looking perplexed. "Well lets' just say his business interest and my business interest don't jive.

All the other whites had the good sense to move out of the area a long time ago, but this stubborn little bastard won't budge. He won't sell out, but above all he refuses to do business with me and my people". Now James knew he was about to thread into extremely dangerous territory with the next question. He wasn't stupid; he realized that this was his crossroad, his point of no return. If the next question was asked and answered; he knew that he would be committed to, but more importantly, indebted to Big Ben Buford.

"What kind of business", James asked.

The sound of the door chime startled young Sonny who was fixated on the story the older Pettigrew was unfolding before him. The senior Pettigrew put down his Cuban and reached for the intercom. "Yeah, who is it". "It's Ellis and Isaiah Mr. P", the intercom answered. The senior Pettigrew got up and headed for the door, "Stay put Sonny", he said staring coldly at his grandson. James sat there for a minute or two gathering his thoughts, when he heard voices coming from down the hall he silently turned off the desk lamp and ever so slightly eased the door open to sneak peek and ear hustle the activity in the hallway.

There stood the old man directing two men dressed in cover-alls; he watched as the men gathered up the body of Sam the Gardener. James was back in his seat when the senior Pettigrew returned. "I know what you're about to ask", the old man said. "Don't worry yourself; Sam will be taken care of as will his family. That's the least I could do since his demise, like you say was my fault. Now where was I" he said as he relit the Cuban.

"My business has many facets" Ben Buford said, looking squarely into the eyes of James. "I guess you could say I'm a public service provider. My organization services the wants and desires of the general public. Those services may include gambling for those who wish to dabble in the games of chance. For pleasures of the flesh, I have a small interest in the world's oldest profession. And for those who wish to partake in a little pharmaceutical escape from reality; I can satisfy that need also. Marijuana, cocaine, and heroin are in high demand out here on the west coast. The potential profits are incalculable and I am determined to benefit from this sure-fire windfall".

"Now this is where we can help each other; I need to be affiliated with some legit businesses to front some of my operations; and old Bernie's would be ideal. You still with me youngster", Ben asked staring that intense glance at James. James poker face, nodded nonchalantly.

"Here is what I propose", Buford continued. "The first thing this morning as soon as he opens, I want you to make the old man an offer. Explain to him how it's been a lifelong dream to open a restaurant in the neighborhood, and since the complexion of the area has somewhat changed over the years; the local gentry is more likely to have a taste for greens and pork chops as opposed to lox and bagels. Make it clear that it might be a good time to sell and move on".

Much to James surprise, he found he wasn't as uneasy as he thought he would be upon hearing such details. Matter-of-fact he felt a rush of excitement with the possibility of becoming involved in Ben Buford's nefarious endeavors, especially with the potential of becoming financially well compensated himself. He did however wonder just how far he was willing to go. He was about to find out.

"I thought you said the old man wasn't interested in giving up his deli", James said leaning forward toward Ben Buford. "Why would he deal with me after turning you down". Ben leaned back in his chair, took a long drag on his expensive stogie and with narrowing eyes extenuating that sinister look said; "In for a penny, in for a pound young blood. Are you sure you want in".

James swallowed hard to erode the rising knot in his throat and nodded. "Yeah Ben, I want in". "Ok Ben said, lets' take a drive".

Chapter 21

MURDER AND THE RESTAURANT BUSINESS

As BEN WHEELED the 1942 creamed colored Packard 110 Deluxe Convertible through the deserted streets toward South Los Angeles, he noticed James admiring the luxurious automobile. "You like" he asked staring at James, "I can't wait until they retool from the war and start producing the new models. I'm on the list to get one of the first ones off the assembly line", bragged Ben. James now knew that he had made the right choice, he envisioned himself enjoying the finer things in life. He would have the clothes, the jewelry, the homes, but above all he would wheel the power to be master of his own fate.

Thirty minutes later they were pulling into the parking lot of a warehouse on South Avalon Ave. Ben honked the horn and the rolling steel door ascended then closed just as quickly after Ben drove inside. James recognized the man who had opened the door; his name was Slim, rumored to be one of Ben Buford's more sinister henchmen. As they got out of the car Ben said something to Slim, then led James to the warehouse office. "Take a seat" Ben motioned to James, pointing to a row of chairs along the office wall. Ben then eased himself into a large black swivel chair behind a beat-up metal desk. James was somewhat surprised at the

handed over the ten thousand dollars in cash that he and Ben agreed should be the purchase price.

As James handed over the cash, he tried to convince himself that this was a good move for the old man and his daughter. If they didn't sell-out; it would only be a matter of time before things got fatal. With ten grand, he told himself that Bernie and his daughter could get out of the area and start a new life in a safer environment. Hell he thought, they may be better off than he was. After all he now was indebted to Big Ben Buford for ten thousand dollars. James collected the documents, assured the old man he made the right decision and that his daughter would be alright, and then left. James never saw Bernie again.

Much later James discovered that in order to get his daughter back; Bernie was instructed to pack all his and Julie's belongings and inform friends and neighbors he had sold his business and was returning to the old country to open a business there. He was then to meet Slim at the Avalon Warehouse and pay a small stipend for his daughter's release; the amount was ten thousand dollars. It was also made clear to James that Bernie and Julie Herzog never made that journey back to the old country. The person who had relayed this information to James was another refugee from the New York crime scene who had been reassigned to the West Coast; his name was Charles "Ice Pick" Charleston.

Chapter 22

ICE PICK

Much to Ben Buford's dismay, Ice Pick Charleston had been sent west to assist Buford in setting up the drug operation. In the intelligence department, Ice Pick wasn't the sharpest suit on the rack but he did know the drug trade and the bosses back east trusted him. At least they knew he would keep them informed of everything that was going on in Black Los Angeles. Not only did Ben dislike Ice Pick, he did not trust him one iota, but he would tolerate his presence to placate the big boys back in the Big Apple. The feeling was mutual, Ice Pick had no love for Ben Buford and he despised Buford's henchmen Slim. That is one of the reasons Ice Pick took a liking to James who also hated Slim; it was one of those enemy of my enemy is my friend, type of relationships. Ice Pick kept James informed of everything that went on. James got more information from Ice Pick Charleston than the bosses back in New York.

Charles "Ice Pick" Charleston was a short stocky man in his forties. Born in Kansas City he was orphaned at age five when his mother died of tuberculosis. He was raised by a number of different relatives who couldn't handle or grew tired of his rebellious nature. By the age of twelve he was living on his own running the streets with one gang after another. Being diminutive in stature was never a deterrence when it came to violence; Charles would take on anyone for any reason, he never backed away from a fight. At eighteen he got into a fight at a wedding; he was talking to an older woman when her husband came in and assumed he was flirting with his wife. The man who was much bigger than Charles managed a few swipes with his straight razor, cutting Charles across the forearm. Charles got his hands on the icepick used to chop ice for the punch bowl and stabbed the man in the throat. Ever since that incident his weapon of choice was an icepick, thus the nickname which he was proud of. In and out of jail over the next decade, he eventually made his way to New York and became an enforcer for one of the large criminal syndicates. He learned the drug trade and was instrumental in promoting marijuana and heroin in Harlem before being sent out west.

Ice Pick though he disliked Buford, did admire his lifestyle and the way Ben Buford carried himself. He thought Ben had charisma and cool; the suits, the automobile, the diamonds, it made Ice Pick want to emulate the man. But try as hard as he did; he just wasn't able to pull it off. The man could put on a thousand dollar suit and still look like he woke up in a corn field. By the afternoon the suit would have food stains on the lapels and sleeves; there would be more wrinkles than a Shar-Pei puppy and he would smell of Jack Daniels. Ice Pick just was not the debonair type; he was definitely a blunt instrument whose expertise gravitated to drugs and violence. James figured he could use that to his advantage.

James was more than successful in converting Bernie's Deli into JP's Southern Soul Food Restaurant, it was the most popular eatery on the avenue, being across the street from the Dunbar attracted all the big name celebrities who hit town. It wasn't long before word spread of its popularity drawing the major black movers and shakers to the front door. And a lot of prominent whites made it a point to drop in at least once a week to rub elbows with the black elite. It got to the point if you were anybody of prominence; your picture was on the wall at JP's. James had to expand twice in three years to accommodate the volume of business he was doing. He was making money hand over fist, but more important he was becoming a pillar of not just the black community, but of all Los Angeles.

The money was good and he had long since paid back Ben, but the profits he was clandestinely accumulating with Buford and his organization thru their drug activity were astronomical. With the flood of money coming in, the restaurant was only able to launder so much; so he started to invest in other endeavors. James opened grocery stores in South and East Los Angeles, and then dove into real estate with a lust picking up properties all over the county. He even opened up a Bail Bond service, the first black owned and operated west of the Mississippi River. James had the politicians and religious leaders eating out of his hand; and nobody suspected his nefarious professional association with Ben Buford and Charles Ice Pick Charleston. Sure he was seen consorting with these people, but James Pettigrew consorted with everyone so no red flag went up. James knew that this would not last forever; eventually he would have to rectify this potentially disastrous situation.

James played the role of silent partner to the tee, but he was well aware of what was going on; he kept his mouth shut but his eyes and ears were putting in overtime. After a while he knew as much if not more about the drug trade as Ben Buford himself, and what he didn't know wasn't difficult to extract from blabbermouth Ice Pick Charleston. He progressed to the point where he could track the journey of heroin from the poppy fields in Indo-China right through the needle of the junkie getting his fix on and everything that took place in between. It was the same with cocaine and marijuana; he knew how the raw material was harvested, manufactured into product, and smuggled into the country. James leaned how the drugs were distributed to the major suppliers and prepared or broke it down for distribution to retailers for consumer consumption.

Above everything else, he understood how the economics worked. It really was not that much different from any other product that was manufactured for consumer use. The price fluctuated based on supply and demand; the demand part was pretty much constant, it seemed as though everyone wanted to get high. On the supply side; when your drug of choice was abundant, the price was low, when it was hard to come by the price went up. Factor in the cost of transportation and smuggling, employee expenses and security, payoffs to public officials and law enforcement, and you were able to figure out an economic formula that worked.

James was ready; it was time to make his move.

Chapter 23

BALDWIN HILLS DRUG BUST

TIME WENT BY and James continued to gain success as a legitimate business man. He met and married the beautiful young daughter of the only black city councilman in city hall, who was a very successful entrepreneur himself. He then purchased a home on Don Miguel Drive in the Baldwin Hills section of West Los Angeles; and as expected the backlash of being the first black family in the area was immediate. His main nemesis was a man named Tom Peters, the president of the Baldwin Hills Homeowner Association.

Peters a construction company owner whose family dated back to the antebellum south was a racist of the worse kind. His father was a high ranking member of the Ku Klux Klan in his home town of Spartan, Alabama. Peters had been raised in an environment of hate and mistrust of any person of color, and he bought that mindset with him upon moving to Los Angeles. Peters and a couple of his cohorts had the gall to pay a visit to James as the movers were unloading the furniture. He made it perfectly clear that they were not welcome in the neighborhood and if he didn't sale and move out by months end; the consequences would be dire.

That very night James was awaken when a brick was thrown through the front window. Upon running outside with the .45 he had bought home from the army, he saw the cross burning in the front yard. It illuminated the whole street in that unmistakable glow of hatred, intimidation, and ignorance that was so prevalent in many areas of the Deep South. The neighbors on both sides and the one living directly across the street rushed to help extinguish the flaming aberration and offer aid; they wanted to let James and his wife know that they were more than welcome as far as they were concerned. Not everyone shared the views of that asshole Peters, one neighbor expressed.

James had an idea; "I'll kill two birds with one stone".

James knew that once a month Ben would send Slim and Ice Pick to an undisclosed location to pay for and pick up that months' shipment of cocaine or heroin. Ben didn't trust Ice Pick one iota; and he didn't give a skunk's ass if the bosses back east trusted the bastard, "Fuck'em". So he made sure that when any money exchanged hands, his man Slim was Johnny-on-the-spot. Ice Pick Charleston was a little dense but he wasn't stupid, he knew Slim was keeping an eye on him and reporting back to Buford; he hated Slim with a passion. "Rat Bastard" is what he used to call Slim when talking to James. James also knew that during the transaction, Ice Pick would check the quality of each shipment by sampling a small amount of product from each package with a testing kit he carried. When all parties were satisfied, the exchange was made and Slim would drop off Ice Pick and then deliver the drugs to the Avalon Ave. Warehouse.

But instead of driving directly to the warehouse, Slim would always stop by the restaurant to have dinner; it was his way of rubbing his position in the organization in James' face. He would walk in like he owned the place, grab the best table and order the most expensive meal. He would then try to glad-hand with any celebrity who happened to be there at the time. Slim would not only refuse to pay for his meal, but he would pick up their tab and tell James it's on the house.

That Friday James knew Ice Pick and Slim were making a Pick up that evening, and sure enough Slim showed up like always. He stopped in around nine-thirty on his way to the warehouse. While Slim was playing big shot, wining and dining some members from the Duke Ellington Band who were performing across the street at the Club Alabam; James made his way out to Slim's car in the parking lot. Like always the brazen bastard left the keys on the overhead visor. James opened the trunk and there under a tarp was four kilos of heroin, individually wrapped just as James had seen at the warehouse. The heroin was wrapped in butcher's paper and clear plastic wrap and secured by duct tape. James removed one package replacing it with one of his own, only instead of heroin his was nothing more than baking soda and brown sugar wrapped identically as the others. He returned to the restaurant just in time for the departing band members to thank him for the great meal and his generosity. James looked over at Slim who was lighting up a cigar and staring coldly back at him. Then James did something that puzzled the hell out of the henchmen, he smiled and walked away.

That next morning as he did every Saturday morning, Ice Pick Charleston stopped in for a good old fashion country breakfast. And James as he did every Saturday sat down and chewed the fat with Ice Pick as he ate his breakfast. When James got up to leave he said, "Oh Charley I almost forgot, tell Slim that we found the briefcase that white friend of his claimed was stolen last night". Ice Pick stopped eating his smothered country fried steak and eggs and with white gravy dripping on the lapel of his suit jacket asked, "What white guy, what the fuck you talking about J.P." "I can't remember the guy's name, Tom something or other", James said. He comes in here maybe once a month or so to have dinner with Slim. Slim never introduced the guy and I never asked, you know how that dick head Slim enjoys his privacy. Anyway one of the waitresses had picked up his briefcase by mistake thinking it belonged to another customer. It's in my office, think you could take it to Slim and have him return it to the guy. "Sure J.P., I'll take the briefcase to old Slim, no problem".

I'll ask, you wouldn't happen to know the white guy's name", Ben asked. "Fraid not" James countered, "He only comes in once a month or so; has a quick bite with Slim and then he's gone, Slim never introduced the guy so I never asked, why is anything wrong". "No everything is just fine, I'll talk to you later", Ben said. "Oh, what did you want to ask me", James said. "Nothing J.P. forget about it, I'll be in for dinner this evening fix up that special gumbo that I like; and oh yeah, Ice Pick will be dining with me"

Later that evening after Ben had departed the restaurant leaving James and Ice Pick alone and still knocking down one Jack Daniels after another, Ice Pick told of how Ben Buford upon hanging up the phone after his conversation with James, walked over to Slim and asked one time and one time only. "Where was the rest of the heroin". "That lying rat bastard was crying like a baby when Ben stuck his revolver in his mouth and pulled the trigger; motherfucker got blood and brains all over my best suit", Ice Pick drunkenly slurred. Since Ice Pick was three sheets to the wind drunk out of his mind, James ordered and poured him into a cab then retired to his office. He was feeling no pain himself as he splashed water on his face, staring into the mirror he said. "One bird down, one to go".

The one to go was one Tom Peters, the president of the Baldwin Hills Homeowners Association. James could have easily rectified the situation by persuading Ice Pick Charleston to pay old racist Tom a little visit. But James wanted to send a less violent but equally profound message to Mr. Peters and the rest of his Baldwin Hills Ku Klux Klan members. So after a couple cups of strong black coffee to help ward off the effects of the Jack Daniels duel with Ice Pick, James retrieved the rest of the heroin taken from Slim and headed for the Westside.

As he drove by Tom Peters' home it was as he hoped; the family had gone for the weekend to Palm Springs. The house was dark with apparently no one home. James drove down the street and parked around the corner. Carefully surveying the neighborhood, he made sure he was unseen as he crept around back and found an open window to the Peters' household. It took no more than five minutes for James to find the master bedroom closet, deposit the heroin in the overhead crawl space, slip out the window, and return unnoticed to his car. James just sat there behind the wheel for a few moments composing himself; he felt no remorse for Slim or for having manipulated Ice Pick and Ben to act as pawns in his little chess game of revenge. No remorse, no feelings of guilt what so ever, he wondered how he could be so cold and emotionless. What was he turning into he thought, then he rationalized that everybody got what was deserved. And that included what was about to happen to Tom Peters.

An unanimous phone call to a police captain James knew was bucking for promotion and a couple of reporters from the Los Angeles Examiner, sat in motion a predawn Monday morning raid on the Tom Peters' household. The commotion of that morning had the neighborhood buzzing for months. The Baldwin Hills residents were roused out of their beds when the LAPD, County Sheriffs, and what seemed like every photographer in the greater Southern California area descended on Tom Peters' house like the seven-year locust. The photographers were going thru flashbulbs at a lightening pace as Tom Peters, his wife, their two children, and his eighty-six year old mother were paraded out of the house in handcuffs.

The police captain who led the raid was telling reporters; how after a long and extensive investigation, his agency was able to bring to justice one of the largest drug traffickers on the west coast. He then proudly displayed the confiscated heroin found on the premises. The scene was reminisce of how big game hunters loved to have their pictures taken with their kill or of those fishermen posing with their catch hanging upside down from the pier hook on the dock.

The police didn't just stop there; they began to question and harass any and every one even remotely associated with Peters. They questioned business associates, friends, relatives, and many of those serving as officers on the Baldwin Hills Homeowners Association. The results were; all those associated with Tom Peters began to distance themselves rather quickly. The Peters household now resembled your worse leper colony; even the milkman and postal carriers wouldn't make deliveries. Tom Peters ended up losing his business and his home after a lengthy and expensive legal battle. On advice from his lawyers, he accepted a pleaded down five year prison sentence, his mother died of an heart attack, and even though his wife was cleared of all charges, she divorced him and moved back to Alabama with the children. The Homeowners Association was disbanded and the first neighborhood watch program was started in its place. The first president elected to the program was none other than James Pettigrew. James even brought the Peters home out of foreclosure and sold it to Ben Buford. As time went by more black families moved into the area and unlike the norm in most other areas, white flight was minimal. The property values actually appreciated at a faster rate than just about any region in the greater Los Angeles area.

One fact was indisputable; after Ben Buford moved into the neighborhood the area reported the lowest crime rate in all of Southern California.

With the demise of Ben Buford's right hand man Slim, James gradually worked his way into a more active role in the organization while maintaining his alter ego of straight laced businessman and pillar of the community. As time went by, Ben Buford and his organization began to separate itself from the mob influence back east; and without much consternation as it turned out. It seemed the crime syndicates were too mired down with other problems. The crime families were at war with each other in the east and the Feds were moving in on their Las Vegas operations. They just didn't have the time or resources to properly monitor what was going on in black Los Angeles.

By the time they had reorganized and began to take inventory on the west coast it was too late. James had helped Buford to develop a self-sufficient organization that operated smoothly and independent of the east coast influence. And they now had the muscle to protect what they had labored to establish. There were some minor skirmishes with a few die-hard east coast hoods who didn't wish to go gently into the night, but Buford and the boys made short work of those efforts. Finally the bosses back east must have said fuck it, it wasn't worth the hassle, let the darkies have Los Angeles. But they did leave a parting shot; some information on Buford somehow found its way to the Federal Authorities. They began a full scale investigation into his activities.

Ben knew he had to be extremely careful with the Feds watching his every move. No loose ends could be left blowing in the wind, all weak links in the organization had to be strengthened or eliminated. And as far as Ben Buford was concerned, his weakest link was one Charles Ice Pick Charleston. Ben could never trust the east coast hood, he instinctively knew if the Feds ever put the thumb screws to Ice Pick, the weak minded bastard would fold like a house of cards and give up everybody.

Chapter 24

LOOSE ENDS, BLOODY HANDS

EVEN THOUGH HE didn't know all the particulars; when James heard of Ice Pick Charleston being fished out of the Los Angeles River, he knew it wasn't a mob hit from back east as initially reported. This was Ben Buford tying up loose ends and just maybe exacting a little revenge from the incident with Slim. James had always felt that Buford didn't completely buy into the Slim drug rip-off scenario. James also knew that even though he and Ben had become close, he could never let his guard down. Perhaps one day he would have to consider Ben Buford a loose end or weak link.

The months passed with Ben managing to stay one step ahead of the Federal Authorities and James was becoming a mega-force on the Southern California business scene. There was even talk of him entering the political arena. But now the Feds were making head way in the Buford Case; they had managed to get their hands on an informant in Buford's crew. Based on this informant's information, the Avalon Warehouse was raided resulting in the confiscation of a large quantity of drugs. The word on the street was that Ben Buford was going to be indicted by the Los Angeles Grand Jury.

James could look right through the street tough, roughneck façade that Ben displayed and see the panic in his eyes. Ben Buford was a hard case and as tough as they come, but the last thing he would ever do would be to serve hard time in prison. He would either go out in a hail of bullets, guns blazing. Or he would cut some sort of deal with the Feds; like maybe offering up a much more tantalizing and higher profile target; a target that would have the Feds drooling all over themselves to bring down. And what could be more tantalizing than bringing down one of Southern California's most successful black entrepreneurs.

Ben Buford himself had just become a major loose end.

Buford had called James the day after the warehouse raid ordering him to bail out the two members of his crew who were arrested. James was fuming, of all the bail bond services in Los Angeles you'd think that dick head would call one I wasn't associated with, he thought to himself. James could envision his entire empire crumbling if his true association with Ben Buford became public knowledge; he had to do something about Buford quickly. But first he had to deal with the two knuckleheads who were arrested at the warehouse.

He made arrangements for their bail and told them they were to lay low while he made more arrangements to slip them out of town. The two hoods picked James up late that night believing he was taking them to a safe house up on Mulholland Drive overlooking the San Fernando Valley. The three of them were laughing as they drove up Benedict Canyon Drive which t-boned into Mulholland at the top of the mountain before dropping down into the San Fernando Valley. One of the henchmen commented. "Here I am a spook from Harlem on my way to hang out in the Hollywood Hills with the movie stars". "Yeah, it can only happen in America", the other thug chimed in as he took a big tug on the bottle of Jack Daniels James had provided. James seated in the back seat said, "Hey pull over in that turn-out there, I have to take a leak".

As the car came to a stop, James had eased out the .45 his camp commander had given him as a gift upon his discharge from the army, and shot each of the two henchmen in the back of the head. He then walked over to the car that was parked at the location earlier that evening and retrieved two five gallon cans of gasoline from the trunk. After soaking down the car and the two bodies thoroughly; he pushed the vehicle over the embankment where it came to an explosive terminus two hundred feet below. James took a quick look around making sure no one had witnessed his little deed. Then he hurriedly got in the waiting automobile his people had parked nearby earlier. He drove off before the sound of the explosion and large fireball attracted attention. Even though the area was extremely remote and secluded, anyone seeing a black man in the area would surely rouse suspicion. As he drove back down Benedict Canyon Drive, James felt an almost euphoric calmness. Tying up loose ends wasn't as hard as he anticipated.

James met up with Ben Buford that next evening at the Club Alabam where jazz great Teddy Edwards was performing. They talked, they drank, they enjoyed the music, and they drank some more. Ben apologized over and over to James about not knowing where those two assholes he had bailed out of jail were. "I told those motherfuckers to go home and stay there until I contacted them", Ben said. "I was in the process of arranging to get them out of the country; but don't worry I'll make good on the money they cost you by jumping bail", he continued. "Don't sweat it Ben", James said. "We can just chalk it up to the cost of doing business, have another drink". James was thinking to himself; get them out of the country my ass, just like you got old man Bernie Herzog and his daughter Julie out of the country. I was gonna get stuck with the bail skip anyway, so fuck it. Ben took another shot of Jack and said. "Well as long as those two pea-brains don't show up, my ass is covered. The Feds got nothing", he said. Then James caught Ben staring at him with a strange look; a look he had never seen before. It was a look James figured Ben didn't know he was making; maybe it was the Jack Daniels or the pressure from the Federal investigation, he didn't know why Ben was staring that weird glance. But James could read his eyes; the look spoke volumes. James could almost swear he could hear Ben Buford saying; "You're next, the last loose end and I'm clear". James knew what he had to do.

Ben decided he better go home before he was unable to drive himself. The business partners exchanged goodbyes at the men's restroom door. But while Ben was shaking off the last drops into the urinal, James was positioning himself on the floor behind the driver's seat in Buford's car. As he lay there, thoughts of what he had done and what he was about to do danced about in his head like surreal images from a dream. It wasn't as though he was doing these horrific acts unmercifully to undeserving and innocent people. He was more or less performing a necessary task to ensure his own survival and well-being. It was like paying a visit to the dentist; you didn't particularly want to do it, but if you wanted to keep eating steak, it was necessary.

Then that conflicted feeling that overwhelms all but the truly insane engulfed James as he hunkered down behind the driver's seat. This feeling resides on a level deep down in the conscious mind; it lives in a place that cannot be corrupted by emotion, logic, or influence. It is where one cannot lie to oneself, even if your life depended on it.

It is the level where Right vs. Wrong dwells. It is the baseline level, the rock bottom level, the no bullshit level. It is the soul's crossroads where the final Right vs. Wrong decision is made. Everyone has seen the cartoon where the little angel is standing on one shoulder, and the little devil is on the other shoulder, both pleading his or her case in each ear. Metaphorically speaking, this level is where those two entities call home. They are just there waiting for your choice, all the arguments and lobbying has taken place, all the debating for each side has ended. It's time for a decision. It's time to act.

Now human nature being what it is; picking Right or Good usually requires little or no further explanation or justification, you just tell yourself it's the right thing to do, you act and move on. But choosing Wrong or Evil is a whole different ballgame. When the wrong or evil choice is made and you know that it's wrong; the justification and rationalizations buffers come into play. "I had no choice, I had to do it" or "It was him or me" or "The devil made me do it" are just a few examples. And for those who are truly honest with themselves when choosing wrong, there is always; "Hell, if doing this is wrong, I don't give a shit, I don't want to be right". This one is probably the most popular; it's usually thought of just before smoking that joint or doing that healthy line of coke, or even meeting at the No Tell Motel. In any event, all these rationalizations and justifications come under the heading of "Guilt Suppression".

James' justification or guilt suppression was the one used in most gangland atrocities; it wasn't personal, it was strictly business. And James Pettigrew was definitely a businessman.

James snapped back to reality just as Ben opened the car door and settled comfortably behind the wheel. The resistance to the ice pick being shoved thru Ben Buford's right ear alarmingly surprised James; he didn't realize that it would be so difficult. Adrenaline flowing, he persisted with as much determination as he could muster. He had a death grip around Ben's throat with his left arm, so as Ben struggled and writhed in pain he was able to keep pressure on the ice pick until Ben became motionless. James looked down; there was blood on his hands.

A major loose end had been tied up; the Feds now had no case and no further leads. James was now in complete control; his legitimate business empire and well-organized drug operation were both his to command. And he had managed to stay in control and unchallenged all these years, until now.

Young James had sat back and absorbed his grandfather's story without interruption. Now that the older Pettigrew was finished he was speechless and not sure of how to process everything he had just heard, he wished that Thelma and Paul were here.

Chapter 25

A WHACKED OUT FANTASYLAND STORY

PAUL WAS SITTING on the sofa watching television while Thelma was standing on the balcony enjoying the view overlooking the Marina, each were absorbed in their own thoughts. Thelma was thinking, just days ago she was working her shift at the Hancock Station Post Office on Vermont Ave. Now here she was standing on the balcony of a professional basketball player's high-rise condo, trying to figure out how to stop a thuggish little hoodlum from turning Los Angeles upside down. And to take the cake, she had come back from the dead to take on this little task. Not even Stephen King would come up with a crazy-ass, bullshit scenario like this, she thought to herself. "But here I am this is really happening"

Paul was channel surfing the sports broadcasts between ESPN and FOX Sports when his cell phone rang. Thelma snapped back to attention and rushed inside expecting Paul to be talking to James. What she heard was Paul asking Detective L.Z. Anderson how he had gotten his cell number. "Who's that", she whispered. Paul covering the mouthpiece said, "He's an Inglewood Detective, but he's a good friend who may be able to help. I don't know why I didn't think to call him earlier". "Andy", who is what Paul had always called Detective Anderson said. "Sure you can come over; maybe you can help me out with a little problem". "A little

Lil G was; no matter how he felt about his grandfather's dark side, he realized that he still loved the man and feared for his safety. "Grandfather all I know is that this Lil G has threatened my associates and me and somehow he has become cognizant of your nefarious business dealings. He is extremely dangerous and will stop at nothing to achieve his goals, just look at what he did to poor Sam."

"And just what about those two so-called associates of yours", the old man asked cutting a glaring eye at his grandson. "Who are they and how do they fit into all of this." "Like I said grandfather, Thelma and Paul are friends who like me found themselves on the wrong side of this G criminal. Paul is a professional athlete who has had run-ins with G over the years, and Thelma has been trying to get the authorities to deal with his gang activities for a long time. And now it's obvious why he targeted me; so he could get to you." "Well Sonny" the old man said, "He got his wish, now I am involved." "I'll handle this little piece of shit; I want you and your friends to stay clear." "Grandfather you don't realize just how sinister this guy is", young James started to elaborate. "Don't worry Sonny I've ridden in this rodeo before, me and my people are more than capable of dealing with this situation". Before the younger James could respond, his cell phone rang.

Thinking it was Thelma or Paul, he answered immediately. "Hey Madison Ave, let me talk to the old man." Startled and without thinking, James handed the cell phone to his grandfather. "It's him."

Chapter 26

H. N. I. C.

Lil G had returned to the club to plan out his strategy for over throwing old man Pettigrew and executing the hostile take-over of his drug operation. Now that everything was in place, it was time to make his move. "Yo pops, it the new **H N I C**," Lil G said to James Sr. I hope your nerdy ass grandson was able to explain everything to you; it seems that boy has a corncob stuck so far up his ass that he has to shit thru his navel. You sure he's from your gene pool," laughed Lil G. "Why don't we dispense with the wise cracks and name calling, just state your business," James Sr. said. "Ok pops have it your way. I know you have a shipment due in tonight; not only are you to turn over that shipment to my people but I want you to convince all of your contacts in Bogotá they are to do business with me from now on". "And if I do this, what assurances have I that you will keep your end of the deal and leave me and my family in peace," James Sr. asked. "Assurances; what do you think I'm running here, Nordstrom or Cal Worthington Dodge, I ain't got no assurances for you pops. I'm a drug dealer just like you; assurances, guarantees, and promises are for those weak-minded nine-to-fivers, not for people like you and me. We operate from a position of power and opportunity; and right now I got the power, you feel me. But I'll tell you what I will do for you," Lil G continued. "Consider this professional courtesy or a retirement gift, whatever floats your boat. You give me what I want and you have my word that I won't bother you and yours ever again. You can live out the rest of your days in tranquility".

"I'll be in contact with the details," Lil G said before the cell phone went silent. "Ok" the older Pettigrew said looking at his grandson. "If Mr. G wants to be the new **H**ead **N**egro **I**n **C**harge, I'll see if I can accommodate him. I have some phone calls to make".

Paul and Thelma were still trying to convince Detective Anderson to call in the Marines on Lil G and his crew, when Paul's cell phone rang. "Paul it's me" said James, "Are you and Thelma alright." "Us we're fine, what about you" Paul answered before Thelma snatched the cell phone.

"James we were worried sick what took you so long to call" Thelma yelled, sounding like a relieved parent scolding a child for not checking in after curfew. "What happened with your grandfather, was the story true, did G call back?" "Jeez Thel, calm down let the man speak," Paul said grabbing her by the arm. Thelma embarrassed by her outburst smiled. "Sorry James go ahead" she said, "What happened with your grandfather."

James upon hearing the concern from his new friends felt an emptiness that he wasn't even aware existed had been filled. At that moment he felt closer to Paul and Thelma then he had to anyone in the past. All the effort to achieve success and stature suddenly didn't seem so important any more. These two people actually cared deeply about him, and the feeling was mutual. He had never let anyone get close before; hell he had not even had a first love now that he thought about it. Even his sex life was purely antiseptic; like one would scratch an itch, or stretch a muscle for relief, but no emotional attachment. Now the three of them were friends for life; however much longer that would be, he chuckled to himself. "James, tell us what happened" Thelma said, snapping him back to the present. "Yes Thelma, everything is true just as Lil G said. My grandfather confessed the whole sordid story and now he thinks he can rectify the situation with G all by himself. You and Paul come back to the estate; I think I may have a plan.

Thelma grabbed Paul by the arm and whispered to him what James had said; they both looked at Detective Anderson. "Andy we have to go" Paul said, "I promise to call you later with more information." "Let me guess, that was contestant number three," the detective said. "What did he have to say?" "Andy you have to trust me, I promise to keep you in the loop. We will need your help, but right now we have to go, please." "Ok Paul, you know that I could haul the two of you in right now for interrogation, but I'll give you the benefit of the doubt. You've never lied to me before, I trust you. But a word of advice; you two better stop by the drugstore and pick up a giant bottle of Listerine." "Huh," Paul uttered, "Listerine." "Yeah to wash out the taste of the big Shit Sandwich you two are about to chomp down on." With that the detective gulped down the last of his coffee and hurried to his car.

Chapter 27

WHAT DO YOU WANT ON THAT SHIT SANDWICH

As THELMA PULLED the Jaguar up to the guard kiosk and let down the window, William stepped out and motioned her to continue through the gate. "Go right ahead, Mr. Pettigrew is expecting you." Detective Anderson, who had been following pulled over to the curb and parked, he knew he couldn't proceed past the security kiosk without rising suspicion with the guard. The moment he drove up and tried to explain his way in; he figured the guard would put two and two together and call with a warning that a police detective was on the way. The detective decided to go into his stakeout mode and wait it out. Besides with the information he had gotten from Dave Marino, he knew they were at the Pettigrew Estate. If they made a move tonight, he'd be right on their ass.

James had just stepped thru the door as Thelma was driving up the long circular driveway. She pulled to stop and James opened the passenger door to help Paul exit the black Jag. "Thanks bro" Paul said, "If things don't work out, you'll make a hell of a valet." James smiled at Paul's comment. "And you sir will make a lousy patron." "Huh" Paul said, looking bewilderedly at James. "No tip homeboy," James shouted." "Where's my gratuity?" Both James and Thelma burst out in laughter. "He got you Mr. Floatin Logan," snickered Thelma. "I think you created a monster."

"Yeah" Paul said, "I guess I did, I can't believe you called me homeboy, what the hell you know about being a homeboy", Paul whispered under his breath as the three entered the mansion.

Big James Pettigrew was standing in the vestibule as Thelma, Paul, and his grandson walked thru the door. For a man in his eighties, he presented a formidable figure. Standing tall, feet spread apart at shoulder width, wearing a black silk robe, he reminded Thelma of Gary Cooper in the old western High Noon, standing in the middle of the street staring down the hired gunslingers. What she didn't know was that Big James standing there looking majestic, right hand in his robe pocket, was again expertly easing the safety off his trusted army issue .45. He had once more shifted into the survival mode that had kept him upright, breathing, and above ground all these years.

"Grandfather these are my friends," the younger Pettigrew started to say. Big James waving his left hand motioning him to be quiet said. "You young lady must be Thelma," he realized right away that she didn't trust or like him one bit. He was able to read her like a book, she wore her feelings on her sleeve and her eyes spoke volumes. He thought she'd make a horrible poker player. "And you young man have to be Paul Logan, the professional basketball player, right." "Yo pops, you figure out all that shit on your own. Your powers of observation are amazing, and by the way that robe is slamming, pull my coat where a brother can pick up one of those." Big James Pettigrew didn't know what to make of this six-foot, four-inch, white boy standing defiantly in front of him mouthing off like nobody's business. For some reason he kind of admired his sassiness. And then Paul said, "Hey pops I can see you seriously strapped, but you don't need to pack that heat in your robe pocket, we the good guys, we here to represent." With that Big James knew that he did indeed like the tall young man, behind all the bravado, posturing, and jive talking the kid was obviously observant and genuinely street smart.

Thelma and young James both went wide eyed when Paul mentioned the gun that James Sr. had cocked, locked, and ready to rock in that robe pocket. "Sorry" said the older James, pulling the .45 out of his pocket and setting it on a nearby shelf. "Force of habit, no need to worry", he said. "Now let's talk turkey shall we, Sonny here will tell you I'm a man that believes in getting straight to the point," as he reached in the other robe pocket for a Cuban. "I assume that everybody knows what's going on here as far as this Lil G character is concerned. He has certain information that could prove, shall we say, embarrassing to my family and me. Now I tried to convince my grandson that all of you should stay out of harm's way and let me settle this, but he is emphatic that the three of you remain involved."

"So unless the three of you can talk some sense into him," he said looking at Paul and Thelma, "I warn you the situation will get a little intense." "You have no idea how intense the situation already is," Thelma shot back sarcastically, "People are being killed and not just criminals and drug dealers but innocent people, for God's sake. Don't you dare lecture us about rather we should be involved or not, we are involved right up to the hilt and that's the way it's going to be."

Thelma for James sake had tried to cover up her contempt for the older Pettigrew, but she was having an extremely difficult time doing so. Thelma had always despised anyone who profited on the misery of others. And as far as she was concerned, there was no bigger contributor of misery than a drug dealer. It made no difference if it was the lower echelon seller on the corner or some big money ass-hole, corporate type whose hands never got dirty. It was unfathomable to her how one human being could knowingly lead another into a life of despair and hopelessness thru drug addiction. And to do so to your own people was almost too much for her to bear.

Paul seeing Thelma's slow simmer escalating toward a major boil, stepped between the two. "That's right pops we in it to win it, that little bastard tried to take out my family so there is no way we sit this one out, feel me. Matter of fact, you better hope we don't drop a dime on your criminal ass after we take care of Lil G." "Alright, I suggest we all settle down," young James interjected. "I believe we are all in agreement that

Lil G is our main concern, so hear me out I have a suggestion that may work."

Lil G was feeling pretty good about how things were starting to come together, all the major competition had been eliminated, the three amigos (Thelma, Paul, and James) were in check, and he had Big James Pettigrew boxed in and ready to turn over his entire operation to TLC. He knew that an extremely large shipment of cocaine was due in that very evening and Lil G had every intention of taking possession of said shipment. Being the only one with a large surplus of product on hand would make him the largest distributor west of the Mississippi. And when old man Pettigrew turned over the Columbians, there would be no stopping us, he thought to himself.

"Hey Smiley we on our way bro" he laughed, looking at his grotesquely deformed henchmen. "We just cornered the nose candy and crack market. After we got every snort junkie and crack head in our pocket, it won't be long before we do the same thing to the heroin pushers. Then I plan to take a run at those redneck Crystal Meth dealing assholes. What'd say Smiley, I guess we'll have to recruit some Tobacco Road Ozark hillbilly motherfuckers to run our Crystal Methamphetamine Division. They can't say I ain't an equal opportunity employer," G laughed.

He then suddenly glared at Smiley, his grin abruptly changing into that sinister scowl that encompassed the embodiment of evil. "I want it all Smiley, I want it all."

Chapter 28

G's Rise to Power

Lil G poured himself a healthy shifter of Hennessy and leaned back in the large office desk chair, he felt a euphoric sense of invincibility. He began to envision the life he had vowed to carve out for himself.

"Tony Montana ain't got shit on me," he chuckled under his breath, referring to the movie Scarface starring Al Pacino. Gerald Lee Henderson had this Nostradamus like prophecy of his future ever since he was a thirteen-year-old junior high school student living in Inglewood. His grandmother gave Gerald the nickname Lil G in reference to his father Gerald Scott Henderson, who was now serving a life sentence for double murder up at Pelican Bay Prison in Northern California. Young Gerald was an extremely bright but street-smart youngster who carried a big chip on his shoulder. To say Lil G was a bad seed would be a major understatement, it seemed that he was always getting into trouble from the time he took his first step.

Being an only child, his mother spoiled him with a lack of discipline while Gerald Sr. considered his sons' rambunctious behavior as a rite of passage into manhood. He would brag to his cronies, "My boy is a bad motor scooter who don't take shit from nobody." After his father's incarceration his mother bounced around from one bad relationship to another, her sense of low self-esteem was a predictable blueprint for becoming totally addicted to drugs and alcohol. Young Gerald was able to cope with the lack of parental guidance and affection; it was almost as if the child was totally emotionless. This concerned his grandmother and other relatives who were alarmed at the lack of emotion he displayed after the death of his mother. She had passed away from a heroin overdose the day after his eleventh birthday.

After the funeral at the repast Lil G overheard a distant aunt say, "That boy has the psychological makeup of Jack the Ripper;" it made him smile and chuckle to himself. When the aunt realized that she had been overheard and made eye contact with the youngster; the sinister smile on his face sent shivers up and down her spine. Old auntie grabbed her purse, uttered a couple of hurried goodbyes, and beat a hasty retreat to her car.

She received two speeding tickets on the drive home to Perris, California. She never attended another family function of any kind.

Lil G's grandmother was a pretty tough old lady who held her own against his rebellious attitude as best she could, but she just didn't have the energy to ride herd over him like she wanted. Regardless she was semi-successful in making sure the boy did go to school. And as painful and boring as school was, Lil G managed to excel in the classroom. That was however when he decided to show up. He spent more time gambling and smoking weed in the bathrooms than he did in class. The boys' vice-principle was constantly threatening him with expulsion for ditching class, gambling, and extorting money from the other students. Much to the delight of the faculty and administration, his class finally graduated and Lil G moved on to high school. He lasted one year before deciding that his formal education was complete and dropped out without ever looking back.

By this time TLC the gang he had formed, was over a hundred members strong and ruled over Inglewood virtually without any competition. They had taken over the crack and marijuana operation from the previous gang who ran most of Inglewood. Lil G had meticulously orchestrated the gangland coupe with laser-like precision. He targeted the main leaders of his competition, who just suddenly mysteriously disappeared. There was no bullet ridden drive-bys, no bloody bodies left lying on the sidewalks, no media coverage, and above all, no police investigating gang war violence. These guys just simply vanished as if aliens or something had abducted them. Lil G knew the usual method of gunning down your competition with the bravado of an OK Corral shootout would only invite retaliation and an escalating body count. That was definitely not the way to keep law enforcement and pissed-off politicians off your ass.

When the rival gang members had realized that Lil G and TLC were the ones responsible for the David Copperfield disappearing act on their leaders, they just knuckled under and gave up their territories. When you have your leaders and half your posse gunned down it creates an aura of martyrdom to inspire revenge. But when they just up and vanish with no explanation, the opposite takes effect. Your own imagination is your worst nightmare; these guys conjured up all kinds of horrific scenarios of which they wanted no part. Most of the older guys left Inglewood, but a great number especially the younger ones figured discretion was the better part of valor, and simply joined TLC.

But it was one episode that cemented Lil G's reputation as a fearless leader and had TLC members talking for years. A rival gang leader from the eastside who was twice Lil G's age, had spread the word that he was going to deal with this little upstart from Inglewood who had the nerve to believe he was the next big shit in town. "Who does this little bastard think he is; you let these young punks pull this kind of bullshit and the next thing you know, you're in the poor house," the elder gangster was quoted as saying. "I'm going to cut his balls off and hang'em around his neck," he continued as he pulled out a brand new, eight inch wood handle, butterfly knife. The knife was a gift presented him by his posse as a birthday present. "That snotty-nosed little shit is gonna be the first notch I crave into this wooden handle," he bragged as he expertly flipped the knife open from its folded position and flipped it closed again over and over.

Early that following Monday morning, the police discovered the body of this well-known eastside gang leader hanging from a basketball pole at

South Park located on South Avalon Blvd. His throat had been cut from ear to ear, there was a note pinned to the zipper on the front of his pants. "I left his intact, this time." According to his crew he was wearing all his expensive jewelry, his wallet was in his back pocket and he was carrying over three thousand dollars on his person; the only thing missing was the wood handle butterfly knife.

Lil G never commented on the incident to anyone but ever since he was seen wielding an eight-inch wood handle, butterfly knife; the knife had a large notch carved into the handle. Lil G figured, sometimes a statement had to be made.

Lil G and TLC were well on their way to becoming a major criminal force in Los Angeles.

Chapter 29

LET'S DO THIS THING

LIL G REACHED for his cell phone and dialed the number he had preprogrammed for the patriarch of the Pettigrew family. "Yo pops, you ready to do this thing," he said as the elder Pettigrew answered.

"Well young man you seem to be calling all the shots, how do you want to work this little transaction," James Sr. answered. "Now that's more like it," Lil G said smiling. "A little cooperation was all I wanted from Jump Street. Here's what you do; make your pick up at the Long Beach Docks as usual. I know that's where the Columbians always meet your people. Then you and one member of your crew drive the shipment over to the Avalon Warehouse; me and my people will meet you there. And when I say you and one member, I mean you and one member of your organization only. I don't have to remind you of the consequences if you suddenly have second thoughts. And make sure you bring me the information on your Columbian contacts in Bogotá. We make the exchange; you give me the Columbian information and the shipment, I turn over the entire original incriminating evidence on you and your family. Then we both have a nice day."

"Don't worry Mr. G I'll uphold my end of the agreement," James Sr. replied. "Just make sure you honor your end, because regardless of what information you may hold over me and my family; I'm still turning over sixty kilos of product that's over a million and a half on the streets and with the contacts you're talking millions more in potential future income. And like you said before, people like you and me are bound by a different set of rules. If certain promises are not kept; believe me I will not go gently into the night."

As omnipotent as Lil G considered himself, the tone and coldness in the old man's voice caused him a moment of pause. The old man had been at this a long time and under normal circumstances, G wondered if he would have the mettle to challenge the old guy like this. "Hey pops just have your ass at the warehouse by eleven with my shipment," Lil G shot back trying to sound just as cold and menacing. He then hung up and took a big slug of Hennessey. Finally he thought to himself, it's almost over in a few hours he would be the number one drug entrepreneur on the west coast.

But timing was critical, just in the short time since he began his coup d'état; there has been a feverish demand for cocaine. The street supply that he had confiscated from his competitors was almost completely gone. The snort junkies were going absolutely ape-shit and were willing to pay damn near any price for the recreational drug. Now he had to hurry and get the flow to the streets going again before any east coast opportunist slid in and started to poach the territory. Since the blood bath, all the local and regional distributors were now looking to him for shipments and he had promised delivery in the next couple of days. No worry he thought to himself, as the Hennessey's soothing effect began to quell the apprehension; the supply and demand equation would swing back in his favor with the acquisition of the old man's shipment. All he had to do was take delivery and verify the quality of the product then have his people break it down and get it to the local distributors. And when the old man's South American contacts kicked in; he would have an unlimited supply from then on. There would be nothing or nobody to stop him.

As Lil G poured the last of the Hennessey into his shifter, he couldn't stop thinking of how old man Pettigrew dared to threaten him. Yeah pops once I got everything I need from you, he thought to himself. I'll crave a special place just for you; as he fondled the wooden handle on the eight-inch butterfly. "Yo Smiley let's roll on over to Roscoe's," he shouted. "We got a little time before meeting up with old man Pettigrew; I got a taste for chicken and waffles."

"Ok Sonny," James Pettigrew Sr. said to his grandson. "Let's do it your way," as he donned his overcoat and headed for the door. Waiting outside in the circular driveway was a panel supply van; the logo on the side read, 'JP SOUL FOOD RESTAURANTS, WE CATER, WE DELIVER.' The driver was a tall muscular black man wearing a salt and pepper New York Apple Cap and an identical Vicuna Overcoat as James Sr.; he hurriedly got out of the van and sprinted around to open the door for James Sr. In doing so he never took his eyes off Paul, Thelma, and young James as they headed for the Jaguar parked in front of the van. "It's alright Roy," James Sr. said. "That's my grandson and two of his friends." "Yes sir," Roy nodded as he diverted his menacing glance from the trio.

While he helped the octogenarian into the van, he said. "Boss it's just unusual for you to be present at a pickup like this; is anything wrong sir." "Nothing we can't handle Roy, I'll explain on the way." James Sr. struggled with the seat beat causing his trusted .45 in his right coat pocket to get caught under his right leg. "Damn contraptions," he said as he rolled down the van window. "Sonny you guys had better hurry, you have to be in place before that G guy gets there. And be careful, you cannot make any mistakes." "Don't worry about us," young James answered back. "Speak for yourself," Paul said while climbing in the back seat of the Jag. Thelma just ignored the older man and slammed the passenger side door hard enough for Paul to scream; "Damn girl."

Chapter 30

WE GONNA BAKE OR WHAT

DETECTIVE ANDERSON WAS working on the forth cup of coffee he had helped himself to from Fire Station 71's kitchen. The fire station was situated directly across Sunset Blvd. facing the Bel Air Estates security gate. While parked in their back yard with the gate open he could see every vehicle that entered and exited the gated community property. One of the firefighters was leaning in the car window to see if the detective wanted to count in for dinner with the guys; all of a sudden Anderson bolted upright and hurriedly started the car. "Gotta go," he shouted at the startled firefighter. "Thanks for the coffee, you guys be safe," he said all in one motion while putting the car in drive and burning rubber through the gate.

The van with the JP's RESTAURANT logo was exiting the gate and turning right heading west on Sunset toward the 405 Freeway, closely followed by the black Jaguar which turned left and headed east. Detective Anderson saw Paul in the back seat with that chick Thelma riding shotgun. The Jag was heavy one additional; the driver, that has to be our contestant number three, Anderson surmised. That must be the lawyer James Pettigrew, he uttered under his breath as he eased the unmarked police sedan into traffic on their six o' clock. "Ok Paul, let's just see where you three knuckleheads are off to," he said while taking a big gulp of Fire Station 71's coffee.

As Smiley pulled the Escalade off Manchester Blvd. into the parking lot of Roscoe's Chicken and Waffles, Lil G was giving final instructions to one of TLC's henchmen. "Just make sure you keep an eye on the placc," he said before flipping close his cell phone. As the two sat and ate, Lil G was having trouble enjoying his usual order; a well-done chicken breast with a double waffle, smothered in strawberry syrup and hot butter. Trying to eat while staring at the hideously deformed Smiley, who was shoveling forkful after forkful of waffles into that unreasonable facsimile of a mouth, was becoming extremely difficult. Most of the other patrons had told the waitress to change their orders to go, or had simply abandoned their half-eaten cuisine and beat feet out of the restaurant.

"Damn it Smiley, slow down asshole," G hissed. "Look at the mess you making." But with no lips, it was hard for the slow-witted Smiley to keep the food from escaping; especially when he attempted to speak between chews. "Hey G why'd you pick that Avalon Warehouse to grab the old man's stash, that's his turf. Ain't you worried about some kind of double cross, I would've had him deliver to one of our pick-up spots," Smiley said while continuing to shovel the banana-nut flavored waffles into his mouth in a metronome like rhythm. Lil G who it seemed was engaged in his own life and death struggle of 'Dodge the Flying Waffles and Syrup Game' which flew in his direction every time Smiley spoke said. "Hey dude I got it covered, I fully expect either the old man or those other three ass-wipes to try something. If they call in Five-O, it'll be his place they raid, not one of ours. And if they try any strong arm tactics or flim-flam moves, we'll be ready. I got one of the crew on point right now checking the place out." "You the man G," Smiley said excitedly launching a large chunk of banana-nut waffle. The syrup covered missile found its mark on the right corner of Lil G's upper lip. "Oh shit," Lil G shouted as the syrup and saliva mixture dripped into the corner of his mouth before he could react with a defensive wipe. "That's it, we outta here, let's go."

"But I ain't done," Smiley protested. "Mofo, you done or you gonna be done," G screamed while trying to spit the acrid taste out of his mouth. "Let's go asshole."

Detective Anderson was having very little difficulty shadowing the black Jaguar driven by young James; matter-of-fact his biggest problem was driving slow enough as to not get too close. Damn this guy sure isn't in a big hurry to get to wherever, the detective thought. They finally made it to Western Ave. and turned right heading toward South Los Angeles. After a mile or so, the Jag stopped in front of a hardware store. James and Thelma went in and purchased a couple of rolls of duct tape and a large roll of dark colored, thick gauge plastic. Upon returning to the car and placing the plastic and tape in the trunk, James realized that Paul had gotten behind the wheel. "Hop in bro, I'm driving" he said. "But what about your ankle," James protested. "My ankle's fine, I'm driving" he said coolly. "No offense bro," he continued, "But you drive like old turtles screw. There's old ladies with walkers passing us up; and like your grandpop said, we have to be finished and in place before that little shit and his people show up."

James looked at Thelma who was trying not to laugh. "Come on James" she said snickering, "Let the jock drive, you know how competitive these athletic types are; you ride shotgun, I'll get in the back." As Paul adjusted the rear view mirror he caught a glimpse of Thelma who gave him a wink and a quick thumb's up. Even James had a slight grin as he slid into the passenger's seat. "Alright you two, I'll acquiesce and surrender to the will of the people." "If acquiesce means you ain't gonna give me any lip service about driving, then acquiesce your ass off. And while you acquiescing find some hip-hop, or some smooth jazz, oldies, anything other than that classical stuff you got us listening to. Your listening habits are like Novocain to the brain" Paul said as he peeled rubber off the curb and darted into traffic.

The sudden change in driving tactics caught Detective Anderson completely off guard; the black Jaguar was now maneuvering through traffic with a purpose. He could no longer navigate and drink his firehouse coffee at the same time. He tossed the Styrofoam cup out of the window and put both hands on the steering wheel. It was now a challenge to keep up with the trio and not reveal his presence. Anderson smiled, now this is more like it, some real police action. He felt like a predator stalking his prey. The game was on and he was excited to play; it had been a long time since he had done any real undercover or surveillance work. His wife Mary had told him, "L.Z. Anderson you getting to old for that cop on the street stuff." Yeah she should see me now, he laughed. Somehow he managed to keep up with Thelma, Paul, and James without being detected; the covert surveillance terminated at 42nd and Central Ave., the site of the original JP's Southern Soul Food Restaurant. Even though the eatery had nowhere near the popularity it had enjoyed in its heyday, the elder Pettigrew kept the restaurant open and functioning on a scaled back level. The cuisine was still old fashion country cooking, but only breakfast and lunch were served. By three o' clock in the afternoon the restaurant was done for the day; the staff had cleaned and locked the place up until the next business morning.

The area had changed demographics dramatically over the years. Where once the city's black population had thrived along the Central Ave. corridor; there was now a majority Hispanic culture. The running joke in the city was that Los Angeles had finally come full circle; the city was founded by Mexico in the mid-seventeen hundred, but after the industrial revolution whites were the majority in Los Angeles proper.

In the early fifties white flight to the suburbs and the San Fernando Valley left South and Central Los Angeles mostly black orientated. By the mid-eighties, the Mexican people with help from their South American neighbors had begun to take back the city one section at a time. If you wanted to get into a heated discussion anywhere in California, Arizona, New Mexico, or Texas; the subject of immigration would be a great catalyst. Conservatives blamed illegal immigrants with everything from government inflation to who shot cock-robin, while liberals abdicated open boarders and amnesty for everyone. The moderates swung both-ways, depending on who was talking at the time. But no matter how you sliced it; the area was now mainly of the Latin persuasion. Even with the change a few remnants of the old black renaissance era could still be found spread around the neighborhood.

The Dunbar Hotel directly across the street from JP's Restaurant had been deemed a cultural landmark; it still stands as a remembrance to an era where the famous and the infamous congregated at the hotel. But now gone were the Club Alabam, the Elk's Hall, and all the other jazz hot spots that used to dot the Avenue back in the day. And even though there is an annual Central Ave. Jazz Festival to commemorate the music that once thrived along the corridor; the present day atmosphere is totally different from that bygone era. That was one of the main reasons James Pettigrew Sr. had refused to close JP's. As far as he was concerned, as long as the Dunbar Hotel remained, JP's Southern Soul Food Restaurant would do the same. It made no difference to James Pettigrew Sr. if the eatery made a dime, it was his start, his launching pad to a better life; it had been his dream. Despite the nefarious circumstances that surrounded the beginning of his success, he could never find it in his heart to close JP's. On many occasions young James had heard his father and grandfather argue over closing the restaurant; his father would extol the value of the land and expressed that James Sr. should at least sale the property if he was not willing to tear down the restaurant and engage in some sort of major redevelopment. He argued that a mini-mall or low to medium income housing would turn a hefty profit that would dwarf the meager income from the restaurant. From an economic standpoint, young James had secretly sided with his father on the issue, but he dared not reveal his feelings to his grandfather.

Now knowing the full truth of how the family success had begun, he wished that his father had been successful in persuading the old man to get rid of the business. He never wanted to see it again let alone setting foot in the place. But now that was not an option, they had a job to do and Paul was pulling the Jaguar into the parking lot of JP's Southern Soul Food Restaurant. Detective Anderson parked on Central Ave. in front of the

Dunbar and watched as the trio retrieved the items from the trunk. They made entry into the now closed restaurant using the keys given them by old man Pettigrew. What were they up to he wondered silently, whatever it was his instincts told him that this was going to be a most interesting evening.

Paul was pouring flour from the large commercial sack into a huge mixing bowl while Thelma was cutting open bags of sugar and baking soda. "Are you sure this is right," he asked looking at James. James looked up from the instructions given him by his grandfather. "Your guess is as good as mine; this is the first time I have attempted to fabricate a batch of counterfeit cocaine." "Yeah no doubt bro, but tell me how in the hell did you come up with this harebrained scheme in the first place." James sat the instructions on the counter and gave Paul a sorrowing look. "Let's just say I got the idea from a story I heard." "Now what" Thelma asked, lying the thick plastic out on the counter. "Cut the plastic into three foot lengths and center them in those baking pans," James read from his grandfather's instructions. "Next we add a little water and a small amount of molasses to the flour and sugar mix to give the substance a hard and lumpy consistency", James continued.

"Jesus H. Christ" Paul shouted. "Why don't we just add some raisins and make oatmeal cookies instead. Is this shit suppose to look like cocaine or Scooby Snacks." "And just what makes you an expert on what cocaine really looks like up close and personal, Mr. Superstar" Thelma asked. Thelma cut a hard and suspicious glance at the tall youngster. "Well go ahead, clue us on how uncut bulk cocaine is suppose to look, mister" "Aw Thel don't go there", Paul said swallowing hard. "I do watch the Discovery and History Channels, you know." "Yeah right, more like ESPN you mean," she answered sarcastically returning to her plastic lining duties.

"Come on you guys, lets finish this up before it's too late; after we wrap this stuff up in the plastic and duct tape it the way grandfather instructed, it should be sufficient for our purposes," James said. After the three had finished pouring their counterfeited cocaine-like mixture into the plastic lined pans and wrapped each one as instructed with the plastic and duct tape; it did indeed look like those images of cocaine confiscated by the DEA and other law enforcement agencies shown on the six o'clock news.

"Ok let's clean up this mess and head for the warehouse, it's getting late" Thelma ordered. Detective Anderson hunkered down low in the unmarked sedan as Paul wheeled the Jaguar out of the parking lot and sped by heading south on Central Ave. The detective whispered to himself, "Ok, here we go again." This time he was prepared for Paul's driving skills and had no trouble shadowing the trio to the Warehouse.

Chapter 31

THE WAREHOUSE

JAMES WAS SOMEWHAT surprised by the appearance of the property after all the years, the warehouse lot looked almost exactly the same as in the photo articles provided by Lil G. The only noticeable difference was the chain link fence which now surrounded the property. The parking lot and loading dock area had that same weather-beaten look; there were small patches of grass and weeds growing through the asphalt at various locations around the exterior of the building. The building itself appeared to be sporting a fresh coat of painted gray stucco that failed to adequately disguise the wear, tear, and age of the structure.

It was as though no matter how thick the cosmetics applied, the true nature of the building could not be covered up. She was an old spinster who refused to accept her aging exterior with grace and dignity. The gray painted stucco was like a coat of that thick gooey pancake makeup worn by the Norma Desmond character in "Sunset Boulevard." And like the actress in the movie, the building seemed to be saying; "Mr. De Mille, I'm ready for my close-up." James giving the building the once over, surmised that one would have a better chance of sprucing up the Pyramids with a coat of Dutch Boy's cheapest, then of making this place look warm and fuzzy. He glanced over at Thelma and Paul and knew intuitively that they felt the same. The building was evil.

There were no indications what-so-ever as to the business identification or ownership on the chain link fence or on the building itself. Other than the "Private Property/Keep Out" sign posted on the fence gate, there was only the address 11801 S. Avalon, hand painted in large block letters over the rolling steel door. Next to the rolling steel door there was a pedestrian door located under a preprogrammed security light which had automatically turned on at dusk. James exited the Jag and quickly unlocked the gate with the keys given him by James Sr. allowing Paul to maneuver the Jaguar onto the property. Paul stopped in front of the pedestrian door and he and Thelma began to unload the counterfeit drug bundles from the trunk. After James had unlocked and opened the pedestrian door, he stood there staring into the eerie darkness.

He held his breath trying desperately not to take in any more of the foul smell which emanated from the depths of the darken warehouse. James was trance fixed almost into a completely catatonic state; he began to sweat profusely as the queasiness in his stomach started to escalate exponentially. Opening that door was akin to a Pandora's Box for James, how many evil deeds had transpired beyond that threshold; the killing of Bernie Herzog, the rape and murder of his daughter Julie, the execution of Ben Buford's henchmen Slim, and who knew how many before and after. Why his grandfather had taken possession of the property after Ben Buford's death; he couldn't understand. James dropped the large key ring and the flashlight he was carrying causing Thelma and Paul to look up from their unloading duties. "James are you alright," Thelma screamed at the younger Pettigrew. Paul seeing the wobble motion in James' stance sprinted over just in time to catch him before he collapsed. "Easy bro I got you," Paul whispered to James as he helped him regain his balance. "I feel you," he continued, "There's some off the hook vibes coming from this place. The car's unloaded why don't you take it and stash it out of sight while me and Thel get this shit inside."

James feeling better said "Good idea I can use the fresh air, don't worry I'll be fine," he continued seeing the worried look on both their faces. "You guys get the packages inside the utility room; the door is on the far wall across from the office, I'll be right back." James handled Thelma the flashlight, closed the trunk, hopped behind the wheel and navigated the Jaguar toward 119th St. He turned right on 119th and parked mid-block figuring that should be a safe enough distance. As he walked hurriedly back to reunite with Paul and Thelma, there were two sets of eyes monitoring his every move.

The first set belonged to Detective Anderson, who had parked his sedan on Avalon across the street from the warehouse; he had observed the entire scenario through the chain link fence. He had absolutely no idea as to what those three knuckle-heads were up to, but his years of investigative police work told him that it was best to wait and see what developed. His only regret was that he had drunk the last of his coffee and there wasn't so much as a fire station, let alone a "Starbucks" anywhere to be seen.

The ownership of the second set of eyes belonged to Petey, one of Lil G's posse members. Lil G had given instructions to Petey to stake out the warehouse and report back if anyone came or went.

At about the same time Lil G was being targeted by the saliva covered waffle missile launched from the lipless Smiley; Petey was calling in to report that some dude and a chick together with a tall white guy had drove up, unlocked the gate, unloaded some plastic packages, ditched their car, and were holdup in the warehouse. "Good job Petey" Lil G said smiling. "Stay on point and keep your eyes open, me and Smiley will be there shorty and the old man should be right behind us. After we're all inside I want you to sneak up quietly and cover our back in case any bullshit goes down, understand." "No problem G, I got it covered" Petey said hanging up. He then reached in his pocket, pulled out and lit up a Jamaican sized blunt. "Might as well get a little buzz on, this waiting and watching is some boring shit," he said to himself.

The blunt rolled in strawberry flavored paper with Petey's own blend of Purple Kush and White Widow Marijuana did its job. Petey was feeling no pain. The car radio sounding good was tuned to 92.3, LA's popular R&B and Hip-Hop station which was spotlighting a remix of Patti Labelle hits. By the time ole Patti got around to her rendition of "If Only You Knew" recorded from a live concert, Petey was on a euphoric cannabis induced cloud nine. He was well beyond a little buzz. "Damn I'm fucked up," he thought to himself. "I better get my shit wired together or G will be carving a notch for me on that freaking knife of his." It was also about that time that marijuana's other side effect kicked in; Petey had a bad case of the munchies. He then remembered the 7/Eleven Mini Mart he had passed on 120th and Avalon on his way to the warehouse. He figured he'd walk the two blocks back to the 7/Eleven, load up on some zoo-zoos and munchies killers, and hot foot it back before anyone showed up; plus the fresh air would help bring his high down.

As Petey was bending over to grab a bag of Flaming Hot Fritos off the bottom shelf and Detective Anderson was putting the finishing touches on his coffee mixture; he noticed the handle of a handgun tucked in the back of the youngster's waistband. The detective who had saw the 7/Eleven marquee from his parked vehicle, and who had also decided to walk to the mini mart rather than risk losing his good parked vantage point to the warehouse, now had a dilemma.

He thought to himself, "Shit this is just great, if this little asshole tries to rob the place and I engage him all hell is going to break loose around here and my surveillance will be blown to shit." Forgetting about his coffee, Anderson cautiously positioned himself behind one of the aisles and reached inside his sport coat unsnapping the strap on his shoulder holster. Much to his delight, the young man never made a threatening move; he paid for the two bags of Fritos, the pack of Twinkies, the three chocolate bars, and the large Gatorade then headed for the door. Anderson blew a sigh of relief but decided to follow the probable gangbanger out to the parking lot. He figured he would write down the license plate number on the youngster's car and radio it in to the county sheriff, it's their jurisdiction he'd let them handle it.

When the detective realized that the guy wasn't getting into a car, but instead was hurriedly walking back toward the direction of the warehouse he loudly said, "You got to be shittin me," causing the store clerk and an elderly woman buying a lottery ticket to both look up startled. "Just where in the hell is this asshole going," he continued as he made his way out of the store not wanting to lose sight of the guy. His instincts had now kicked into an even higher gear; somehow he surmised that this gun toting jack-off maybe tied into what was going on at the warehouse. Sure enough his suspicious were true, following the youngster back to 118th Street Anderson observed him getting into a car parked almost directly across from the gate leading to the warehouse parking lot. "Well I'll be damned, this little shit was stocking up for a stakeout." Anderson upon returning to his own sedan checked his 9mm. Glock and the .38 snub-nose backup he carried in his ankle holster. He reached into the glove box and retrieved a pair of binoculars. From his vantage point he could make out the gate, the parking lot, the warehouse doors, and young Mr. Gun-in-the-waistband stuffing his face with Flaming Hot Fritos. Then it hit him; he had left his coffee at the 7/Eleven. "God damn it; now I'm really pissed," he said loudly. "Somebody is going to get his ass kicked tonight."

Roy was now northbound on the 405 Freeway; the pickup in Long Beach had gone as smoothly as ever. The only concern was with the Columbians who had made the delivery; they were somewhat surprised that James Pettigrew had been in attendance. It was extremely unusual and rare that someone of his stature would be present at a shipment drop.

Roy who usually handled shipment deliveries had assured them that everything was on the up and up, that Mr. Pettigrew just wanted to get out and review some of the operations. The Columbians had the upmost respect for the American businessman; he had visited their country many times as the guest of their leaders. He was a man of his word who could be trusted. Even during the violent regime of Pablo Escobar's cartel leadership, James Pettigrew managed to conduct business with virtually little violence. His personal relationship with government and military leaders of the country had made this possible. He had complete autonomy as a businessman in South America and was probably the only American that Pablo Escobar and the cartel truly respected and maybe even feared. He and his people had been doing business with Mexico and South American dating back to the forties, his reputation and business dealings with the reigning leaders was impeccable. Everyone in the organization knew if anyone tried to pull any kind of shenanigans their bosses would deal with them extremely harshly. So Roy's explanation was accepted at face value and the sixty kilos of pure cocaine was transferred to the van without any further ado.

James Sr. had briefed Roy on what was going on with Lil G and his grandson while driving to Long Beach, he said that he personally wanted to make sure that the shipment would be packaged the same as usual. He had given explicit instructions to Paul, Thelma and his grandson on how to create and package the bogus drugs to look like an exact replica of the Columbian shipment. If they were to fool Lil G, it had to be perfect. Roy a suspicious man by nature who had been with James Pettigrew Sr.'s organization for over twenty years wasn't sure this was the best way to handle the situation, but he respected his boss's decision. "Come on Roy speak your mind," the old man said. "You think this is a bad move, don't you." "Well sir it's just that your grandson has never been in this kind of situation before. And what do we really know about those two friends of his; this whole thing could be some kind of trap. They could be misleading your grandson and be in cahoots with this Lil G fellow."

James Sr. sat expressionless as Roy continued; "And besides pulling a switch on this guy is going to accomplish diddley; even if he turns over his evidence once he discovers that we rooked him, he will come after us. "Yes Roy I've thought of that but I have been dealing with guys like him for years. It's my gut feeling that this is an all or nothing move on his part.

He's so sure of himself, so confident that he has the upper hand and that makes him vulnerable. I'm sure he'll have all the evidence with him just to throw it in my face and gloat if nothing else. But I do expect that he will renege on his promise, he's the type that has to be the big cheese in town, so he wouldn't be satisfied knowing that I was still around. That's why you're here Roy, be prepared in case our plan goes to shit. I just want to make sure my grandson and his friends get out of there all in one piece, that's the number one priority, understand." "Yes sir," Roy answered. "You can depend on me." "Good" the old man said.

"Now here's what's going to happen; once we pull into the warehouse make sure you back the van up with the ass end facing the utility closet on the west wall. My grandson and his two friends should be inside with the fake product. After this G character inspects the shipment I'll get him over to the office where we can exchange the Columbian contacts for the evidence he's holding against me. While we're making the exchange; that should give Sonny and his friends time to make the switch and slip back into the utility room without been seen. Hopefully everyone will go his separate way and then we can deal with him later. If not I have one more ace in the hole that should get us all out of there in one piece." As Roy was exiting the Century Blvd. off ramp on the Harbor Freeway, James Sr.'s cell phone rang. "Yo pops, I'm just about at your warehouse I suggest that you get there pretty damn quick," Lil G ordered. "Patience young man," answered James Sr. "We'll be there in ten minutes." Lil G hung up without answering, Smiley made a right turn off Avalon onto 118ᵗʰ St. driving right pass L.Z. Anderson's unmarked sedan. The detective immediately recognized Lil G riding in the passenger seat of the gold colored Escalade; he slumped down in the seat and focused his binoculars on the Caddy as it stopped opposite the vehicle that Mr. Flaming Hot Fritos was in. "Ah shit things are about to get funky," he murmured to himself.

Petey got out of his car and walked around to the passenger side of the Caddy. "Any new developments" Lil G asked staring straight ahead not looking at Petey. "Nope" replied Petey, "Just those three I told you about; they unpacked some packages from their car, from here it looked like a shipment of smack or something. The white boy and the chick carried them inside while the brother drove the car around the corner before coming back on foot.

He then locked the gate and went inside with the other two." "You sure nothing else," Lil G asked coldly finally turning to look at Petey. "You were keeping a close watch, right." "No doubt G," Petey managed with false bravado desperately hoping that Lil G didn't detect the pungent order of the king sized blunt he had finished earlier. "I'm Sharp Eyed Washington, steady on the case G, ain't nobody in there but those three assholes I told you about; hell beside them you the first car that even came down the street since I been here." "Ok" G relented, "The old man and the blow will be here any minute; now get out of sight and wait until we're all inside then I want you to get the AK, ease your ass up to the door and check out what's going on. Any bullshit goes down; you open up first and ask questions later, got it." Petey nodded, returned to his car and drove down the street to an alley inlet about forty yards from Avalon Blvd. and backed in facing 118th St.

Detective Anderson observing the whole scenario decided to continue to wait a while longer before making any kind of move, he figured as long a Lil G was parked outside the gate and Mr. Flaming Hot Fritos was holed up in the alley, Paul and his two cohorts were probably safe inside the warehouse. It was obvious that everyone was waiting for someone else to show. Sure enough one minute later a panel van drove pass and turned onto 118th St., it drove down the street and stopped at the gate entrance facing the Caddy Escalade which had parked on the wrong side of the street just pass the gate facing back toward Avalon. The two vehicles were parked facing one another bumper to bumper. Through his binoculars Anderson could make out the two drivers exiting their vehicles. Inside the warehouse, Paul peering through the window on the pedestrian door was watching the same scenario. "Ok guys it's game time" he said and the trio headed to the utility room.

As Roy and Smiley walked toward the gate, Lil G and James Pettigrew Sr. stared unblinkingly at each other through the windshield from their respective vehicles. The dimly illuminated interiors of the Caddy and the panel van added to the eerie and suspenseful aura that emanated around these two determined, desperate, and dangerous men. Like two heavyweights boxers sizing up each other before the bell rang; each was looking for a chink in the other's armor.

Both men refused to be the one that blinked first. Finally being in each other's presence, this was indeed the first true test of wills between the two drug lords. Despite the age and physical difference between the two; this first encounter had to be considered a push.

James Sr. immediately recalculated his impression of the young man, his ability to read people told him that this guy was not to be taken lightly. He was indeed a hungry young man; James Sr. could see the burning ambition in the young hoodlums' eyes. It was a look he was familiar with, it was the look he himself had when he first came to Los Angeles years before. Sonny was right; he thought to himself, this guy is dangerous.

Lil G could feel the majestic presence of the old man as they stared at one another. Then his jealousy meter pegged out at maximum; there sitting not ten feet away was what he had envisioned for himself for years, a man who had it all. It was not particularly the wealth or the material things that Lil G graved, what he wanted more than anything was the power and the respect that men such as James Pettigrew Sr. commanded. Strangely and much to his dismay, no matter how hard he fought he failed miserably to suppress his admiration for the old gentlemen. They both were oblivious to everything else taking place around them as the stare down continued. Then the sound of the gate sliding open snapped both of them back to reality.

Roy returned to the van and drove through the gate toward the warehouse. "Goddamn sir, did you see that ugly son-of-a-bitch," referring to Smiley. "That's one gruesome looking mother; what in the hell happened to his ass." James Sr. didn't comment. Smiley followed the van through the gate and parked. He and Lil G watched as Roy entered the warehouse via the pedestrian door, turned on the lights, and opened the rolling steel door entrance. They then followed Roy inside as he backed the van in with the rear facing the utility closet door as planned. Roy helped James Sr. out of the van then closed the rolling steel door assuring their privacy.

Lil G approached James Sr., "Ok pops we almost done but first things first. We all know everybody here is strapped, but this is suppose to be a straight up business transaction. Let us all agree to keep our hands in plain sight, there's no need for violence." James Sr. smiled, "That's very astute of you young man, I agree whole heartily.

Let's get this over with and call it day, I assume you will want to check the merchandise." "You assume right old man," G answered. The four men went to the back of the van, where Roy unlocked and opened the door. Lil G hopped into the van and removed the tarp covering the kilos of cocaine. Each was wrapped individually in dark brown plastic and bond with standard duct tape. Lil G using his butterfly knife randomly chose three packages and began to remove a small sample of the drug from each. He then retrieved a testing kit from Smiley and tested the purity of the three packs he had chosen. "Yo pops my hat's off to you, this is some good shit I got it testing out at a high percentage. Smiley grab another couple of keys and double check me," G said grinning from ear to ear. Smiley confirmed the results. "Yeah G this is the purest blow I ever seen, the dealers can step this shit down over and over and still have potent product, we gonna make a grip and a half."

"I assume that you're satisfied with the merchandise," James Sr. said. "I suggest that we retire to the office and conclude the rest of our business." "No doubt pops, lead the way," Lil G said making sure he and Smiley were trailing James Sr. and Roy. The office was on the opposite side of the warehouse separated by three large pane glass windows which allowed viewing of the warehouse floor from the office area. The windows had louvered venation blinds that provided privacy between the warehouse floor and the office if desired. The blinds were fully extended down to the window sill, but were still slightly open allowing a limited view between the two areas. James entered the office and turned on the light, followed closely by Roy, Smiley, and Lil G who closed the door behind him.

Lil G then laid the small briefcase he had been carrying down on the worn wooden desk which faced the office window. Roy stiffened a bit and mentally prepared to reach under his overcoat for the Glock in his waistband when G started to open the briefcase. James Sr. standing there unflinching calmly reached out and grabbed Roy's arm in a reassuring manner. "Here it is pops everything I have on you. The photos of you and Ben Buford, the bail bond certificates, the newspaper articles, the affidavits from Bernie Herzog's family in Israel stating he and his daughter never arrived, and private logs from Ben Buford outlining his business dealings with you before he came up dead. It's all here just like I said."

"Very well" responded James inspecting the material. "Now how about satisfying an old man's curiosity, just where did all this information come from." "Come on now pops," Lil G said laughing. "I heard you were a pretty good poker player; when you get an opponent to fold you don't show him your hand. Now how about those Columbian contacts, let's wrap this up."

James reached into the inside upper pocket of his overcoat; this time it was Smiley who started to react defensively. "Easy old man" the deformed posse member ordered while reaching for his own weapon. "Chill out" Lil G ordered. "Pops is a man of his word, stand down." James pulled out a small envelope and handed it to G; inside was a folded piece of paper with one phone number on it. "What the fuck is this," Lil G shouted. "Calm yourself" James said. "I'm a man of my word remember; that phone number is all you'll need to conduct business with the South Americans. These people are extremely cautious, you didn't really think that they would just take my word for it that they should take you as a man that could be trusted. It's taken me years to gain their trust and respect as an honorable businessman, and that's something that you will have to earn on your own. Believe me, just getting you that phone number tells them that I vouch for you.

But out of respect, it will be their decision to do business with you. The ball's in your court, what you do with it is up to you. If you can't handle it; maybe you're in the wrong business. I'll tell you what," James Sr. continued. "I like your enthusiasm and you show a lot of grit, why don't you come and work for me. I can have Roy here show you how things are done and maybe in four or five years you'll be ready to take over his duties, freeing him up to replace me. James was deliberately baiting the young gangster, he could see his anger rising. His plan was working, James wanted to make sure that Lil G's attention was focused right there in the office; not on the warehouse floor.

At about the time that James Sr., Roy, Smiley, and Lil G had closed the office door, Paul, Thelma, and young James had unlocked and were quietly easing their way out of the utility closet just to the rear of the panel van. "Finally some fresh air, it's stifling in that closet," Thelma whispered. "Ok if this bullshit scheme is going to work, it's now or never," Paul said quietly. "I can't believe that I'm actually pulling this head fake on a bunch of murderous drug dealers," he continued.

"Hold on" young James said. He was feeling much better after hearing his grandfather conversing with Lil G through the closet door. Their conversation had caused an adrenaline rush that helped abate the previous apprehension he experienced. "Let me check something out before we make the switch." He then stealthily made his way into the rear of the van. "What the hell" Paul said looking at Thelma. "Who does he think he is now, James **Bond**". Thirty seconds later James returned to the closet. "Paul let me see that knife you took from the restaurant." They then began to carry the bogus drugs from the closet to the van. It took no more than a few minutes before they had finished moving the kilos from the closet into the van, and then the kilos from the van back to the closet.

Petey flicked the AK-47's safety to the off position; from his vintage point at the pedestrian door window he had witnessed the trio's little exercise. He then snuck into the warehouse and positioned himself behind the Caddy, making sure he had a clear field of fire if they came out of that closet shooting at G and Smiley when they exited the office.

Lil G was glaring at James Sr.; "Fuck you old man, you're done I don't need you throwing me crumbs. I'll have those South American assholes eating out of my hand in no time. And as far as me working for this piece of shit flunky of yours," referring to Roy. Lil G with amazing speed pulled his butterfly knife out of his jacket pocket, flipped it open and savagely swung at the much taller Roy's neck. The butterfly found its mark severing both the carotid artery and Roy's trachea in one powerful swing. The only sound Roy was able to make was a small gurgle noise before dropping to his knees clutching at what remained of his throat. After the powerful swing of the knife; the flow of blood was enormous. With each diminishing beat of Roy's dying heart, blood squirted in all directions covering the desk, the floor, and James Sr. who with his own surprising speed and agility for such an elderly man had knelt down beside his fallen confidant and was desperately attempting to render aid.

Roy now supine on the floor stared up at his boss, the life in his panic stricken eyes slowly began to flicker and fade away, his bloody grip on James Sr.'s overcoat sleeves loosened and his hands finally dropped to the floor causing the pool of blood to splash droplets onto the sadden face of James Sr. Though no sound was emitted, he silently mouthed the words, "I'm sorry boss," then he died.

The senior James mentally snapped back to reality as Roy closed his eyes for the last time. In a fit of rage he reached for the coat pocket which housed his .45, but before he could free the firearm, Smiley had his own nine millimeter's muzzle firmly planted against the back of the older man's head. "Easy old dude" Smiley said excitedly. "I'll take that." He reached in James Sr.'s pocket and retrieved the firearm. "Hey nice piece you got here, old dude. Hey G can I keep this," he said. "You cowardly little bastard," James Sr. hissed at Lil G. "Shut up old man or you'll be joining that piece of shit on the floor there," he answered back.

"If you do that, the shipment out there in the van will be the last you'll ever see," James said gathering his composure. Lil G narrowed his eyes and tightened the grip on the butterfly. "What the fuck you talking about old man," he asked while staring daggers at the senior. "That phone number I gave you is useless unless a special code word is used in conjunction. And that information stays with me until I'm safely at home with this evidence. Do we understand each other, you sadistic little punk," James Sr. spat at Lil G. "Is that right," Lil G answered smiling that sinister grin of his. "We'll see about that;" he motioned to Smiley, "Let's go." Lil G led James Sr. and Smiley through the office door onto the warehouse floor.

"Ok you three assholes, you got five seconds to show yourselves before I ghost the old man," he screamed as loud as possible. James Sr. gulped hard trying to hide his nervousness. "Who are you yelling at," he asked. Petey jumping up from his cover position behind the Caddy shouted, "You know damn well who he's yelling at, they're in that room behind the van G." Lil G began to count loudly, . . . one, two, three, four. The utility room door swung open. "Alright, alright," young James hollered at Lil G. "We're coming out, please don't hurt my grandfather." "That depends on you," Lil G said. "You wanna explain what you assholes are doing hiding in that closet." "We were looking for the Watts Towers and got lost," Paul sarcastically shouted back. "Hey nerd pack," Lil G said looking at young James. "That white boy is gonna get your grandpapa smoked with that smartass mouth of his. "Paul be quiet," Thelma said tugging on the ballplayer's arm.

"Hey G they pulled some kind of switch, I saw the three of them moving bundles back and forth from the closet to the van after you guys went into the office," chimed in Petey. "Good looking out Petey, I knew they would try some sort of bullshit move. Keep that AK pointed at the old man's head"; he then entered the closet. A few moments later he emerged from the closet and hopped in the van, in even less time he climbed out of the van and returned to his original position behind the elder Pettigrew. "Tell me you assholes didn't think I'd be dumb enough not to figure out a flimflam move like this. Smiley you and Petey get the coke out of the closet and load up the Caddy, they switched out the whole load while the old man had us in the office. You can still see the knife marks in the packs where we checked the quality; nice try pops but no cigar. Now if you want to see your stick-up-the-ass grandson and his two friends walk out of here, you'll give me that code thing that goes with this phone number. You know the drill, I'm counting to five." He then looked over at Petey who had finished helping Smiley load the coke bundles from the closet into the Caddy and nodded. Petey took aim with the Ak-47 automatic rifle pointed at young James, Thelma and Paul. "One, two, three, "Don't tell the bastard shit," yelled Paul. "He can't hurt us." "Four," continued Lil G. **"VENGANZA,"** yelled James Sr. "The code word is venganza; when you dial the number you will be asked for the code word. You will then be transferred to a person who will ask you how much product and when and where you want delivery. You will discuss a price; once terms are agreed on you'll be given an account number to a bank in the Cayman Islands. Upon delivery and your satisfaction with the product you will transfer agreed upon funds to that account number without delay by the next business day.

This system is based on actions by honorable business people and has been in play for many years. If you are less than honorable in any phase of these transactions; if you fail to transfer the agreed upon funds, or if you instigate any violence what-so-ever. You will not be able to buy so much as a pound of chili powder from any Mexico or South American affiliates, ever. And that's only if you survive the carnage that they will unleash on you and everyone even remotely close to you. Now let my grandson and his friends go."

Lil G was ecstatic, he had finally reaped what he had toiled so long to achieve; now nothing or nobody could stop him. In a very short time he would be the most powerful underworld drug figure on the west coast. His visions were no longer delusions of grandeur, but a reality that was about to come into full fruition. "Ok pops I believe you, but I think I'll hold on to you just a little bit longer, just to make sure this number and code thing is legit," Lil G said. "Now you other three cockroaches get into the back of the van." He directed Petey to get the keys and lock

Thelma, Paul, and young James in the back. "Where are you taking my grandfather," protested young James. "If you three don't get in there, I'm taking him out, that's where," G answered.

After Petey locked the van door, Lil G said. "Once we leave drag the stiff from the office and put him in the driver seat then cut the gas line and torch this thing off. When you're done meet us at the club." Lil G didn't really know if setting the van on fire with Paul, Thelma, and James inside would actually get rid of the three, but it would certainly put a major hurt on them. I mean just look at what happened to Tray and Smiley, he thought. "Ok Smiley let's roll," he ordered.

The Caddy pulled out into the parking lot heading for the gate. The car sped right past Detective Anderson who was crouching down by the pedestrian door, gun drawn. The detective had made his way up to the building just after Petey had made his entrance. He had been able to hear most of the conversation from his vantage position, but had decided to wait for an advantage. If he made a move too soon, Thelma, Paul, and both of the Pettigrews would be in the line of fire. Now that advantage had presented itself, Petey armed with the automatic weapon wasn't expecting any interference. Anderson made his move just as Petey started toward the office to retrieve Roy's body. "Stop right there, drop the gun and turn around with your hands above your head," the detective yelled loudly at Petey.

Petey stopped in his tracks but the experienced law enforcement officer could read his body language, he steadied his aim. The front sight of his Glock would focus dead center between Petey's eyes when he made a turn. The whole scenario began to decelerate before the detective's eyes; he was seeing everything move at an hourglass pace, but he was still functioning in a digital time frame. It's that moment where highly trained individuals can anticipate and react before their opponents realized what happened.

"Don't do it young man," Anderson yelled firmly but with as much compassion as he dared allow. "Drop the gun, son." Petey wheeled attempting to level the AK-47 in the direction of the detective's voice; the business end of the Glock roared to life. Two shots were fired, both found their mark. The first by itself would have been fatal, but the detective wasn't taking any chances. A weapon like the AK-47 could wreak wide spread mayhem if the young gangster had managed to open fire, not only he but those inside the van could be hit. Detective Anderson had no choice; it marked the second time in his career that he had to drop the hammer on a man. He briefly reflected on the psychological ramifications that would come later, but right now he had to stay focused. His job wasn't finished.

Inside the van Thelma jumped and gasped a frighten sigh upon hearing the gunshots, no matter how many times she had heard the sound of gunfire since moving here from Louisiana; the sound never failed to send a chill down her spine. Then the rustling of keys in the van door now had James and Paul on edge as well. "Are you guys alright," Detective Anderson asked while holstering his gun. "Holy shit Andy, am I glad to see you" Paul said with a sigh of relief. "What was that shooting, who got smoked, it wasn't G was it," he asked rapidly. "No it wasn't Henderson, it was one of his crew," Andy answered "They took my grandfather," James said jumping from the van. "We have to do something." "Calm down" the detective said, helping Thelma climb out of the van. "I overheard where they were going. They'll be at that club he owns over on Sepulveda. But first let's get a few things sorted out; right now I've got two dead bodies. One I'm responsible for; the other looks like the work of Gerald Henderson. Second, there's a prominent businessman that has been kidnapped and from what I heard; we have a van full of bogus cocaine that you three so called con artist failed to switch for the real thing. Somebody had better explain to me what the hell is going on, and do so most forthwith."

"Sir if I may," said young James. "Let me explain the nature of our predicament." "That means he'll try to make a long story short," interjected Paul and Thelma in unison. James began again, "You see detective, truth be told my grandfather has been involved in illicit drug trafficking for numerous years. Now this G Henderson fellow has taken it upon himself to forcibly wrest control from my grandfather and his organization through extortion and murder.

"I see," said Anderson; "Now what's the story with this scam drug switch scheme." "It was our intention to see to it that Mr. Henderson received no compensation what-so-ever for his extortion of my grandfather and family. If we were successful, the drugs would be turned over to the proper authorities." "And your grandfather," Anderson asked. James could not look the detective in the eye. "Obviously he'll have to pay for his indiscretions," James muttered. "Come on Andy," Paul said. "We trying to do the right thing here, cut us some slack." "And just what made you amateurs think you could pull off a con like this; now Henderson has not only your grandfather but also a million dollars' worth of cocaine." "Not quite," Paul said smiling.

James and Paul drug the box holding the kilos of cocaine out of the rear of the van. James then removed the top row of the wrapped packages revealing the five kilos that Lil G and Smiley had tested earlier. "I don't understand" said Detective Anderson. "If this is the real drug shipment, what the hell got loaded in Henderson's SUV." Paul laughing and patting young James on the back said, "Let's just say if that asshole G wants to have a bake sale, he's well on his way. The only high anyone will get off that shit he took is a sugar rush." Paul was roaring with laughter now, Thelma was starting to giggle and even James had managed a small grin. Paul between belly laughs explained their phony concoction made to look like cocaine to the detective. "But they saw you make the switch," Anderson said. "No, what they saw was us moving the fake coke into the van; James then used a knife to cut holes to resemble G's testing holes in five of the fake kilos. Then we took the fake packages back out of the van and returned them to the closet." "Mr. Smart Ass Lil G out foxed himself," chuckled in Thelma.

"Slick move" the detective said, "Which one of you Ice Berg Slims thought this up." "James gets the credit," Thelma answered. "Actually I got the idea from a story my grandfather told me. Also I observed the young man that you just vanquished sitting in his car on my return to the warehouse after parking my car. I surmised that he was probably affiliated with Lil G and was assigned to watch the warehouse and report on all activity. It was a calculated risk, but faking the switch seemed to be the most prudent course of action.

But we did not anticipate my grandfather being taken hostage." "Don't worry," interjected Anderson. "I'll have LAPD's Swat Unit at Henderson's club before he does anything to your grandfather, Lil G Henderson is ruthless but even he doesn't want a bullet up the ass. Believe me, he'll give up I know him." Paul grabbing the detective by the shoulders said. "No, no you don't know him Andy; things are different now, he not worried about getting smoked anymore."

"What are you talking about, what is it that you three aren't telling me. There's something strange going on here and you guys are starting to really piss me off." "Andy it's too complicated to explain right now. You've trusted us this far, just hang with us a little while longer, please." Paul was on the verge of begging. "We have to handle G ourselves." Detective Anderson stared at Paul, Thelma, and James his analytical mind and police training told him to secure the scene, call for backup, and have units respond to Lil G's club hangout. But his gut feeling persuaded him to go along with these three. It was almost as though a feeling of euphoria had descended over him assuring that trusting in these three individuals was the right thing to do. "Ok Paul I will probably regret this, but we'll try it your way."

"Well Mr. Pettigrew have you got another mission impossible like plan in that trick bag of yours," the detective asked. James looked at the detective, but said nothing. "How about you two," he asked again looking at Paul and Thelma. They also were quiet. "Just as I thought," he sighed. "Ok, here's what we're going to do."

Chapter 32

VENGANZA

"I'LL GET THE car keys off our departed young hoodlum there," referring to the lifeless Petey. "We'll use his car since Henderson and his people are expecting him," Anderson said. While Thelma, Paul, and James walked down the street to retrieve Petey's car parked in the alley, Anderson took a mental inventory of the warehouse and the events which had taken place. He knew he would catch hell for not following proper procedures when this little adventure came to light. "What the hell," he said to himself. "I probably won't live through this charade anyway." He then locked the warehouse doors and the gate to the parking lot. "Move over I'm driving," he said to Paul when they met him at the front gate. Paul upon settling into the passenger seat looked at the detective and said. "By the way Andy, we saved you a piece." "A piece of what," responded the detective. "A piece of that shit sandwich you told us about," laughed Paul.

"Smart ass," responded Anderson. "First stop is that 7/Eleven; somebody owes me a cup of coffee."

Smiley turned the Caddy into the rear parking lot behind Club West, the building was empty except for two of Lil G's posse members. They had emptied the club as ordered. "Any problems," Lil G asked as they walked over to the Caddy. "Nope, we told everyone we were closing early for repairs just like you ordered, G." "Good, now help Smiley unload this coke and then you two takeoff, I'll be in touch in the morning. Leave the gate open for Petey, he'll be here shortly. Ok pops let's go," G said grabbing James Sr. by his overcoat's lapel. "You can make yourself comfortable in my office." "What do you want from me," asked the elder Pettigrew. "You got everything you asked for, and what of my grandson and his friends." "No need to worry about them; you better worry what's to become of yourself if this phone number and that code bullshit doesn't work like you said." "Don't worry young man; it'll work just fine," James Sr. responded.

"We'll see," G said pouring himself a hefty shifter of Hennessy. "Oh excuse my manners, can I offer you a libation." "No thank you," answered the senior looking at the young gangster with distain. "You can choke on it." Just then Smiley and the two posse members walked in with the last of the kilos. "G we out," the posse members said. "Ok Smiley start storing the coke, the guys can pick it up their shipments in the morning; we back in business bro."

As the two posse members drove through the gate and their tail lights faded down the street, Detective Anderson cautiously turned into the parking lot. Having told his three passengers to lay low in their seats he maneuvered Petey's vehicle with the headlights facing toward the windows on the rear of the building. Smiley glancing out the window could just see the make of the car through the headlights' glare. "Petey's here G," he said unlocking the door then returning to his duties storing the kilos in the hidden panel behind Lil G's private bar.

"You three stay put," ordered Anderson as he exited the car gun drawn. "If anyone drives up honk the horn and stay out of sight." He then hurriedly made his way to the door and entered, he figured if he moved fast enough maybe he could surprise the occupants before they realized he wasn't the recently departed Petey. The rear entrance opened up to a narrow hallway, up ahead on the right was the door leading to Lil G's office. The detective could hear Lil G talking to James Sr., it was now or never. He tried the door knob, the door eased open; he could make out Lil G sitting at his desk with his feet up sipping on a large brandy shifter.

James Sr. was sitting on a couch directly across from the desk, looking disheveled and worn. The Inglewood Detective never saw the grotesquely deformed Smiley bending behind the bar storing the kilos of cocaine.

Detective Anderson burst in with his Glock trained on Lil G. "Don't move Henderson," he shouted moving toward James Sr. "Look out," the elder Pettigrew tried to warn. A shot rang out, Anderson felt an intense white hot pain in the rear of his right shoulder blade, the Glock flew out of his hand and skidded across the tile floor. Smiley standing behind the bar was leveling the .45 back into firing position, taking careful aim at the downed Inglewood Detective. "Hold on Smiley," yelled Lil G jumping up spilling Hennessy all over the desk.

He walked over to the fallen detective who was face down on the floor writhing in pain; G grabbed Anderson by the wounded shoulder and turned him over. "I'll be damned; it's that Inglewood cop that's been on my ass since forever. What the fuck are you doing here," Lil G asked kicking Anderson in the wounded shoulder. The detective screamed in pain. "You're under arrest asshole," he said after catching his breath. "Yeah right I got your arrest," G answered. "Smiley get this piece of shit up and put him on the couch next to pops." Then the door burst open a second time. Paul, Thelma, and James rushed in; Paul's athletic muscular torso sitting on top of those long basketball player's legs was able to transverse the distance between the door and Smiley before the hideous henchmen could hardly turn his head. "Get away from him you ugly bastard," he shouted. He then slammed a well-aimed right cross into what was left of Lil G's number one henchmen's grossly deformed face.

The surprised Smiley was knocked backward into Lil G causing both to fall onto the top of Lil G's desk. Lil G slid off the side of the desk onto the floor, but Smiley recovered and reached for the .45 he had tucked into his waistband. But before he could bring the weapon to bear on Paul, Detective Anderson had been able, even thru immense pain, to pull the revolver out of his ankle holster and fire all six shots point blank center mass into the chest of Smiley. Smiley fell backward over the desk and onto the floor. With his smoking revolver now empty, Anderson started to retrieve his Glock laying against the far wall. Then to his disbelief and horror, Smiley reappeared from behind the desk with the .45 pointing directly at him. Paul yelled "No", just as Smiley pulled the trigger.

Detective Anderson closed his eyes waiting for the inevitable, he quickly thought about his children and grandchildren. Then he summoned up a vision of his wife; "Sorry Mary I won't be home tonight," the thoughts flashed by. But then he felt the pressure not of a bullet, but of something much heavier. James Pettigrew Sr. had flung his body between the bleeding detective and the henchmen, just as Smiley fired. The older man groaned in agony and slumped heavily to the floor at Smiley's feet. Lil G, up from the floor stopped Smiley before he could fire again.

"Oh no," screamed the younger Pettigrew tears swelling in his eyes. "Why, why," he sobbed clutching at his gasping grandfather. "Sonny, please forgive me," the elder man gasped. "I only wanted the best for my family, and to make life a little easier for all of you. Please forgive me for not showing you how much I've cared for you and how proud I am of you. James Pettigrew Sr. died in his grandson's arms before young James could give his forgiveness.

Lil G snatching the gun from Smiley said, "You three are like cockroaches that won't go away, just what in the hell do I have to do here. It's over, I won accept it," he continued. "This town belongs to me." "Bullshit," yelled Paul as he started to advance toward G. "That gun won't do you any good remember, I'm going to whip your ass until Judgment Day." Lil G then took aim at the wounded Detective Anderson, who was still staring at Smiley. The ghastly looking Smiley was standing over him with six still smoking holes in his gray hooded pull-over sweatshirt. Anderson could see that he wasn't wearing any protection underneath the pull-over. How could he still be breathing let alone standing there. The old man who had saved his life was laying dead at his feet still being held by his grief stricken grandson, and now Lil G Henderson had him at gunpoint. What had he gotten himself into; this nightmare couldn't get any worse he thought to himself.

He was wrong.

Lil G said, "Maybe I can't kill you three assholes but if you don't back off me, Inglewood will be less one detective." Young James pulled himself away from his grandfather and took a stance between Lil G and Detective Anderson. Thelma and Paul quickly joined him forming a human shield around the wounded police officer. "So now what," Lil G laughed. "I told you it is over." "Is that what you think," asked James. "Just what have you won nothing that's what. Did you really check the drugs that you took from the warehouse." That sinister smile of Lil G faded to a look of semi-shock; he tossed the .45 to Smiley. "Watch them, if they move run over there and put one behind the cop's ear," he ordered. He had his butterfly out and was slashing at one of the kilos laying on the office bar's countertop. Ripping open the plastic wrapping he placed a small sample of the white substance on his tongue. The acrid taste and numbing sensation associated with the drug was missing.

Instead the substance had a sweet flavored taste. Lil G in a panic pulled out and tested the kilos already stored, the results were the same. "Oh yeah," Paul said gleefully. "Gotcha Mr. Big Time Drug Lord, the only people that have to watch out for you now is 'Famous Amos' or maybe 'Betty Crocker'. That win that you thought was there, is now missing like Jimmy Hoffa". Lil G was furious he couldn't think straight. Smiley more in control than Lil G said, "Hey G we got the old man's connection, remember. We can replace the stash." Lil G's panic suddenly escalated, he ripped the number out of his pocket, grabbed the desk phone and dialed.

"Operator 42, code word please," came the reply on the third ring. "Venganza", G said loudly. "Hold on please," a female voice replied with a Latin accent. After about five seconds a male voice answered. "DEA Agent Martinez, code word confirmed, phone trace completed, will begin surveillance on all shipment locations; good work Agent Smith." Lil G's expression went blank, the color drained from his face. James glared at Lil G, "My grandfather always said to keep your associates close, but keep your adversaries even closer. He always knew where, when, and what the officials were doing when it came to his business. He kept this little DEA surprise on tap in case he ever needed it. So enjoy my grandfather's little gift; also in case you didn't know, **Venganza** is the Spanish word for **Revenge."**

Lil G ripped the phone wire out of the wall and screamed, "I'll kill you, you motherfuckers" and darted toward James. "Smiley blow that cop's head off," he ordered. But before anyone could move the room went icy cold; a nauseating odor settled over the inhabitants, an eerie red tinted light began to illuminate over the entire office. As the light began to intensify the large office desk just vanished into nothingness. In its place now stood the tall hooded robe garbed figure that had given Lil G his mission after the car crash with Paul.

It was Big Spooky himself hovering over Smiley and Lil G. **"Failure will not be tolerated,"** resounded in everyone's head in a clear and crisp tone. Lil G looking up into the faceless hood pleaded, "No I had it all, it's not fair they tricked me, I can fix this, please no." He then looked over at Smiley, who had suddenly burst into flames. It wasn't the white hot inferno that previously sent Tray into oblivion, but a slow burning red and yellow fire that seemed to dance and pulsate to an unheard rhythm. There was no sound of any kind, no screams of pain from the fully engulfed Smiley.

The only thing visible was the .45 which he held in his right hand, the weapon seemed to float there for a few seconds and then dropped to the floor undamaged; Smiley was gone. The flame began to decrease in intensity to where all that was left was a single line of fire along the floor. That single line of slow burning flame then began to eerily creep toward Lil G. He attempted to run but the only muscles that were not paralyzed controlled his eyes. They were wide and darting back and forth in a panic. Thelma who was staring at Lil G surmised that those eyeballs would jump right out of the gangster's head and beeline for the door if they could. His mouth was formed to emit a scream but no sound escaped, he then managed to focus those panicking eyes on the approaching flame which was now at his feet and gaining intensity again.

The red and yellow flame lengths began to encircle Lil G in a counter clockwise motion. As the flame completed its circumference around G's Timberlands, it began to rise from his feet toward his upper torso. When the circle of flame reached Lil G's shoulders, it started to rotate faster and faster until a vortex of red and yellow light illuminated the room. The only thing visible other than Lil G's head bobbing and weaving above the swirling inferno was the butterfly knife he still held in his right hand. Suddenly the churning red and yellow conflagration fully encased Lil G leaving the butterfly knife suspended in midair just outside the cocoon of flame. It hovered there for a few moments before it started to slowly melt into a mixture of molten slag and burning wood. The swirling vortex of flame then began to ebb in intensity as the now unrecognizable butterfly knife dropped to the floor. The instant Lil G's murderous knife hit the floor, the circle of red and yellow fire dissipated into nothingness. There was no sign of Gerald "Lil G" Henderson. The ruthless little gangster was gone as though he never existed. There was virtually total silence.

The only sound heard was that of Detective L.Z. Anderson's heavy breathing, he could hardly feel the pain in his shoulder. He was dumbfounded as to the events unfolding before his eyes. He had always prided himself on being an open-minded individual. Being a police detective required such an attribute, but this was ridiculous. He then looked up at the giant hooded figure that was now facing him, Thelma, Paul, and young James Pettigrew.

Wiping the sweat from his eyes, the detective wondered if he was two blinks away from insanity. As the four of them huddled before the ominous-looking hooded aberration, not moving and hardly breathing; two pinpoints of light began to sparkle inside that black abyss-like hood. The tall figure began to glide in their direction. "Oh shit", Paul yelled. All of a sudden a brilliant white florescent type light appeared between them. Stepping out of the brightness was Gus.

"I don't think so," he said looking up at the tall menacing creature. The hooded figure Lil G had named Big Spooky stopped and looked down on the much shorter Gus. "Go ahead," Gus said staring up and into that ominous hood. "Make a move, we've been here before." Big Spooky began to tremble in an apparent rage, then turned and vanished just as quickly as he appeared.

"Way to go Gus, my man," Paul said excitedly. "And thanks for looking out for my family, I owe you bro." "God bless you Gus," Thelma said planting a big kiss on his cheek. "Yeah, he usually does," Gus said laughing. "I'm sorry about your grandfather James," Gus said wrapping his arm around the young Pettigrew. "But take comfort in knowing that he died doing a noble and unselfish deed, and considering the life he led; that will go a long way in determining how he is judged by powers higher than me. But just between you and me, I do have a little influence. I'll see what I can do."

"Now what do we do about you," Gus said looking at Detective Anderson. "I suppose you have a few questions as to what's going on here." L.Z. Anderson who had finally convinced himself that he was not dead or had a sixties flashback, said "Well sir, to tell you the truth, I don't know where to begin. Just tell me if I've lost my mind." "No detective, you are as sane as I, but you are privy to an extraordinary turn of events. I will explain if you think you can handle it. But beware if you accept, you may be called into service again in the future; otherwise I have the ability to make you forget all that has taken place, it's your choice." "I think I can handle it," Anderson answered. "Good," Gus said "Because these three will need all the help they can get." "Does that mean we get to stay," Thelma asked. "Yes, you three did an outstanding job," Gus answered. "The boss thinks you can do a lot of good, so you get to stay. Gus then explained the whole scenario to Detective Anderson.

"Let me make sure of one thing," the detective said. "I am still kicking right". "Yes sir, you are quite alive, and with no conditions what-so-ever", Gus answered. "Good because if I don't get some help for this shoulder, I'm not going to be alive much longer", he said grinning and winching at the same time. "I can help you with that", Gus said placing his hand on the detective's wounded shoulder. In an instant, Inglewood Detective L.Z. Anderson's shoulder was as good as ever and he felt great. "Now for your first mission detective; you are going to have to explain all this to the authorities." "The authorities, I'm still trying to digest all this myself. How am I going to come up with something believable that'll keep me out of the rubber room or worst out of jail myself" " I never said it would be easy detective, use your imagination," answered Gus.

"Now you three better get out of here, the less anyone knows about you, the better for everyone," Gus said looking at Paul, James, and Thelma. "You all will be hearing from me shortly," Gus continued. Then he was gone. "Welcome to the team Andy," laughed Paul. "Detective, you may regret your decision," chimed in James. Thelma said, "Ok, guys let's get outta here, anybody hungry. I feel like cooking. Detective, we'll look for you at my place when you're done; I'll save you some Blackberry Cobbler." "Not if I can help it you won't," said Paul. "Just don't eat all the Gorilla Bread," said James. "Gorilla Bread, its Monkey Bread you dipstick," laughed Paul. "Man, I don't know what we're going to do with you, dude."

Detective Anderson just smiled as he watched the three walk out the door. "Just save me some of that great coffee."

EPILOG

THE BATTLE BETWEEN good and evil continues. The ongoing confrontation will rage on and on wherever mankind congregates. Most will agree that the human race as a whole is basically good, but evil is ever present and will manifest itself every chance it gets. Some will say that evil is the necessary component that balances the equation of life. That good cannot exist without evil. That it has been this way since the beginning. For argument sake, say this is true; then the battle lines are drawn.

Each side will vie for dominance and the armies that serve these two forces are forever recruiting.

The Southland now has three new inductees, three diverse individuals who came together to utilize a common bond of decency and courage to prevent evil forces from turning Los Angeles upside down.

While Paul, Thelma, and James were successful in their baptismal confrontation, the opposition will not cease in its attempt to tip the scales in their favor. The ever present evil forces are planning an even more sinister scheme to leave the City of Angels in ruin.

Gus has faith in his new recruits and now with Detective L.Z. Anderson, one of Inglewood's finest on the team, he will not hesitate in calling upon their services.